TAKE THE
MUMMY
AND
RUN

THE RIOT BROTHERS SERIES

TAKE THE MUMMY AND RUN

The Riot Brothers Are on a Roll

by MARY AMATO
illustrated by
ETHAN LONG

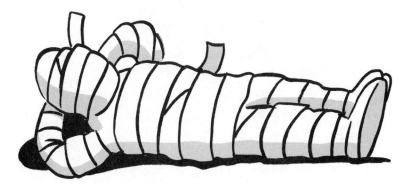

Holiday House / New York

Text copyright © 2009 by Mary Amato
Illustrations copyright © 2009 by Ethan Long
All Rights Reserved
Printed in the United States of America
www.holidayhouse.com
First Edition
1   3   5   7   9   10   8   6   4   2

Library of Congress Cataloging-in-Publication Data

Amato, Mary.
Take the mummy and run : the Riot Brothers are on a roll / by Mary Amato ; illustrated
by Ethan Long. — 1st ed.
p. cm.
Contents: The Riot Brothers solve a mystery — The Riot Brothers find a lost
mummy — The Riot Brothers have fun at a water park — Bonus.
ISBN 978-0-8234-2175-6 (hardcover)
[1. Brothers—Fiction.   2. Cousins—Fiction.   3. Summer—Fiction.
4. Humorous stories.]   I. Long, Ethan, ill.   II. Title.
PZ7.A49165Tak 2009
[Fic]—dc22
2008013299

For my Riot Brother fans with thanks
to the Albion family—especially Zoe, Noah,
and Michele—for sharing the idea of Amelia.
—M. A.

For Alec and Ashley.
Love, your bro.
—E. L.

CONTENTS

Book One
THE RIOT BROTHERS
SOLVE A MYSTERY

Book Two
THE RIOT BROTHERS
FIND A LOST MUMMY

Book Three
THE RIOT BROTHERS HAVE FUN AT A WATER PARK

TAKE THE
MUMMY
AND
RUN

ONE
Don't Stop
the Pop!

Ahhhhhhhhh, the first day of summer vacation! The beginning of fun and freedom for me, Wilbur Riot!

I woke up and decided to start the day with a bang. So, I lunged toward my brother Orville's bed.

My goal was to wake Orville up by pulling

his pillow out from under his little head. Unfortunately he woke up at the exact same time with his own idea.

We headed toward each other like meteors on the same flight path.

Kapow!

"Ow!" Orville said, rubbing his head. "Your head is as hard as a rock, Wilbur."

"I'll take that as a compliment, Orville. I've always loved rocks. Your head is as hard as a giant kernel of popcorn. Before it has popped, of course."

"Thank you, Wilbur!" Orville cried. "I've always loved popcorn."

He started popping around the room as we got dressed.

"This is making me hungry," Orville said. "Let's see if Mom will let us make puffers for breakfast."

Puffers is Orville's nickname for popcorn. He came up with it when he was three, and it stuck.

"And then we can start our summer off by playing Pufferbelly Pointer Punt," I suggested.

"Hooray! I love that game!" Orville cried.

We popped down the stairs.

"Mom!" Orville yelled. "Can we make puffers for breakfast?"

She wasn't in the kitchen or the living room. "MOM?" I yelled.

Orville looked worried. "Do you think she finally went nuts and is now running through the streets of town squawking like a chicken?"

I looked out the window. "I think she's gardening."

Orville joined me at the window. There was good old Lydia Riot, otherwise known as Mom, kneeling in the dirt, talking to herself and waving one bright purple gardening glove in the air.

"Well, maybe she has finally gone nuts."

Orville opened the window and called out, "Mom, can we make puffers for breakfast?"

She waved at us. "Shhh! I'm on the phone."

"She said, 'Yes! Leave me alone,'" Orville said with a grin.

We put some popcorn in the microwave and waited patiently. With every *pop, pop,*

pop, the delicious hot bursty smell increased. Yum . . . Yum . . .

Ping!

Finally, the timer went off and the popping stopped.

We tore open the bag, poured those white fluffy puffers into a bowl, and ate as fast as we could.

"Time for Pufferbelly Pointer Punt," Orville said. "What's your team name?"

Coming up with a team name is an important part of Pufferbelly Pointer Punt. "This time I'm going to be the Wilbur Weirdos," I announced.

"Good choice! You will be playing against the Orville Uh-Ohs."

He held out his pointer finger. We locked fingers and shook twice.

"All rise for the Pointer Anthem," I said.

We stood up, put our pointer fingers in the air, and sang,

O say, can you see,
our pointers with glee?
What so proudly they stand,
as a part of the hand.
With their knuckles they bend;
they're the thumb's closest friend.
They help us to write
by holding our pencils.
They point out the way;
they can wiggle and sway.
Although they can't snap,
they are quite good at tapping.
O say do they bravely dig wax
out of our ears.
So let's raise our number ones!
Now this anthem is done!

We took our places across from each other at the dining room table and put a puffer in the center.

"Go!"

We went for it. I was first to the puffer. I flicked it from one pointer to the other. Orville tried to steal it, but I punted it up the field. Aiming for Orville's belly button, my outstretched pointer struck it—*ping!* Right in the middle of his stomach!

"GOAL!!!!!!!!!!!!!!!!!!!!!!!!!!!!" I cried, while my pointers did a victory dance. "One point for the Wilbur Weirdos."

"The game ain't over," Orville said. He put another puffer on the table and we went at it again.

This time, Orville got it first. Without hesitating, he shot it. *Pschew!* It shattered into pieces and flew over my head.

"Out of bounds. The Weirdos get a free kick."

I got a new puffer and placed it perfectly. I needed to catch the Orville Uh-Ohs off guard. Quickly, I flicked it.

"NOOOOOOO!" Orville screamed, and

punted in midair. The puffer parachuted down and smacked me in the stomach.

"GOAL!!!!!!!!!!!!!!!!!!" Orville's pointers did a victory dance. "Uh-oh! It's one to one, baby."

I reached for a new piece of popcorn and noticed all the unpopped kernels hanging out together in the bottom.

"Orville," I said. "I know we're supposed to be playing Pufferbelly Pointer Punt, but I'm suddenly distracted by an important question."

"You're wondering why we aren't wearing knuckle guards?"

"No. I'm wondering why are there always a few kernels that don't pop."

"It's a mystery," he said.

An idea popped into my head. "I've got our next mission!"

"Does it have to do with puffers?"

"No."

"Good. I'm full."

I waved my fingers mysteriously in Orville's face and said in a mysterious voice, "The Riot Brothers will solve a mystery."

Orville held up a piece of popcorn. "About puffers?"

"No. A real mystery of some kind. Something that takes two things that we've got."

"Pointers?"

"No. Courage and intelligence. Otherwise known as guts and brains."

"I've got guts and brains!" Orville cried, punting a piece of popcorn into the air. "Mystery, here we come!"

TWO

Who Wouldn't Love Slobber in a Bucket?

Mom came running into the room. "Guess what?" she asked.

I looked at the popcorn on the table. "You're going to yell at us for playing with our food?"

"No. Although that reminds me: You guys need to stop leaving the shed door open. Three days in a row, I've noticed that it's been wide open. But guess what?" She was actually smiling.

"You're taking us to China for our summer vacation?" Orville asked.

"No."

"You're *not* taking us to China?" I asked.

"No! I mean yes. I mean—"

"Mom. Are you or aren't you taking us to China?"

"Of course I'm not."

"Then why do you keep talking about China?"

Mom rolled her eyes and pulled a Riot Rewind.

What's a Riot Rewind, you ask? It's a little something we invented, which our mom even finds handy. To do a Riot Rewind, you pull both ears and say, "Rewind!" Then you back out of the room while making your voice sound garbled, as if you're talking backward. After that you get to come in and have a fresh start.

Mom stopped when she got out of the room. Then she ran back in.

"Guess what?" she asked, but she didn't wait for us to answer. "Your cousin is on her way. Your second cousin, actually."

"What cousin?"

"The one who is coming to stay with us while her parents attend that conference in the hotel downtown. Remember I told you about this two weeks ago?"

Our mom talks so much it's hard to keep track of what's important.

"Older or younger than us?" I asked.

"In between the two of you."

"Nice or mean?" Orville asked.

"Nice, I'm sure!"

"Not all females are nice, you know," he said. "Did you know that only female horse-flies bite?"

"No, I didn't," Mom said.

"And only female mosquitoes bite," Orville added. "Did you know that?"

"No, I didn't," she admitted.

"Boring or funny?" I asked her.

Orville interrupted. "Wait, Wilbur. Are you asking about horseflies or mosquitoes?"

"I'm asking about our cousin, Orville. Is she boring or funny?"

Mom put her hands on her hips. "How am I supposed to know? We saw her once when she was two. Wilbur, you were three. And Orville, you were just starting to walk."

"Well, was she funny?"

Mom laughed. "As a matter of fact, she

was. We were at a park with a lot of pigeons, and she found a feather on the ground and kept running after a pigeon trying to put the feather back on."

Orville laughed.

"Can she do any tricks?" I asked.

"You'll have to ask her."

"What if she won't talk to us?" Orville reasoned.

"Why wouldn't she talk to you?"

"Maybe she only speaks Chinese."

"She's from Kansas!"

"Well, why didn't you say so!"

Mom's eyes went for another roll.

"When is she coming?" Orville asked.

"Any minute. They arrived last night and stayed at the hotel together. And they just called to say that Amelia is on her way here."

"Who's Amelia?" Orville asked.

"Your cousin!"

I interrupted. "The important question is, when will she leave?"

Mom went nuts. "Wilbur! That's not nice. She is going to be our guest for three days, and the two of you will be excellent hosts, I'm sure."

"THREE DAYS!" I wasn't really trying to be mean. It's just that it was the first day of summer vacation, and I didn't want to be stuck taking care of a boring guest.

Orville turned to Mom. "So, what do hosts do?"

"They chitchat, Orville," I said. "And they show their guests where to freshen up."

Mom laughed.

"Perhaps we should buy some candy and new games for excellent hosting." Orville fluttered his eyelids.

"Forget it," Mom said.

I whispered, "How are we going to keep our mission a secret or even complete it with a guest hanging around?"

Orville nodded, getting it. "What should we do?"

My brother directed his question at me, but it was Mother-With-Big-Ears who answered. "The first thing you should do is sweep the floor," she said. "It looks like you guys were throwing popcorn around in here."

I guffawed. "Of course not. We wouldn't *throw* popcorn—"

"We *punted* it," Orville said.

For some reason, Mom didn't see the

logic of this. Sometimes trying to explain the concept of fun to grown-ups just doesn't pay.

While I was sweeping unpopped kernels of popcorn into a dustpan, I got a brilliant idea.

"These kernels remind me of peas," I whispered to Orville. "And peas remind me of the story of the princess and the pea." I dumped the kernels into the trash can. "And that gives me an idea."

Orville looked horrified. "You want to dress up like a princess?"

"No. I want to create a test for our cousin to see if she's the kind of cousin we like."

"Aha!" Orville said. "We'll make her sleep on a bed full of peas!"

"No. We're not trying to find out if she's a princess. We're trying to find out if she's *fun*. So we'll play a funny trick on her, and if she laughs, then we'll like her."

Orville's face lit up. "Bingo bongo! What'll we do?"

Too bad I can't sell tickets to my brain because sometimes the ideas just roll in there like little movies.

I told my plan to Orville, and then we carried it out.

First, we put Slobber in a bucket full of water. (Note: Slobber is the name of our pet rat, who happens to be made of rubber. If you think it's disgraceful that we do not have a real pet, then please write a letter to our mother, Lydia Riot, explaining that children need at least one dog, one cat, one iguana, one Burmese python, and one naked mole-rat in order to grow up and become normal healthy adults. Thank you.)

Second, we put the bucket on the front step, next to the door.

Third, we put a sign on the bucket saying, FREE CANDY!

Fourth, we walked to the driveway to see how it looked. From a distance, you could see the bucket and the sign, but you couldn't see what was floating in the bucket.

"Perfect," I said. "Now, she'll walk up to the front door. The sign about the candy will make her look in the bucket, and then she'll see old Slobber!"

Orville did what any good Riot Brother would do. He laughed like a madman.

THREE
A Rather Curly Surprise

We wanted to hide in the bushes and wait for the cousinly arrival. But Mom made us clean more. And then she asked us to look for her missing gardening glove.

I was checking the bushes by the Overhosers' house when Mrs. Overhoser came out.

She gasped. "Are you tromping on my petunias?"

"No. I'm just looking for a missing glove," I explained.

"Hmph!" she said. "I'm missing a glove, too." She pulled one blue gardening glove out of her apron pocket and looked at me suspiciously.

"I didn't take it," I said.

All she said was "Hmph." *Hmph* is the Overhosers' favorite word.

We didn't find any gloves, but all that looking made us hungry again. So, we went inside and made peanut butter toast. While we were eating toast, we made a list of possible mysteries to solve.

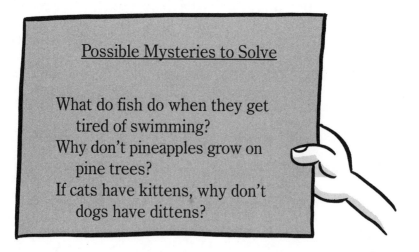

Possible Mysteries to Solve

What do fish do when they get
   tired of swimming?
Why don't pineapples grow on
   pine trees?
If cats have kittens, why don't
   dogs have dittens?

Before we could even finish our list, the doorbell rang. I looked at Orville. Orville looked at me. We had forgotten about the test we'd set up for our cousin.

"Slobber!" I tried to say, but my mouth was full, so I ended up slobbering. We jumped up and ran into the living room, where we bumped into Mom.

"She must be here," she said.

"But nobody screamed," Orville said.

Mom gave us a look. "Why would anybody scream?"

"Yes, why would anybody scream, Orville?" I poked him with my elbow.

We ran to the front door and peered through the window.

Nobody was standing on our steps, and a taxi was just pulling out of our driveway.

"Uh-oh," I said. "Maybe we scared her off."

Mom tapped me on the shoulder. "For heaven's sake, why would she be scared?

Maybe the taxi is confused about the address. Just open the door, Wilbur."

Orville and I opened the door and . . . guess what happened?

You'll never guess, so I'll just tell you.

We opened the door and a long green snake fell on our heads!

"Aiiiiiiiiiiii!" we screamed.

A skinny girl wearing an old aviator hat with short funny hair and a huge grin jumped out from behind our bush. "Gotcha!"

It's hard to stun the Riot Brothers, but stunned we were.

Mom stepped forward. "You must be—"

"Amelia!" the girl said. She picked up her rubber snake. "And this is my pet snake, Curly."

I looked at Orville. Orville looked at me.

"A girl with a fake snake," Orville whispered. "I think she's our kind of cousin."

FOUR
What's in Your Backpack?

Talk, talk, talk. It's all grown-ups want to do.

How was the trip? Are you hungry? How have you been?

They don't even know how to ask good questions.

Do you have any candy? Can you do anything funny with your nostrils? Was there a mini-fridge in that taxi? These are good questions.

Mom was asking question after question, and frankly, time was wasting.

"Pardon me for interrupting," I said in my excellent host voice. "We need to show Amelia where to freshen up."

I gave Amelia my secret Riot Brother wink.

Right away she got it. "Yes," she said. "I obviously need freshening."

"Looks like we've got three peas in a pod here," Mom said with a big smile.

Before Mom could talk more about vegetables, we grabbed Slobber and Curly and led Amelia into the backyard.

"I like your style," Amelia said. "What are we going to do?"

"We need to have a secret Riot Brother meeting," I said. "We are the Riot Brothers. And according to Riot Brother Rule Number Twenty-Four: Kids who are fun can become Riot Brothers even if they aren't our brothers."

"Did you just make that up?" Orville whispered.

"Yes," I whispered back.

He gave me a thumbs-up.

"Would you like to join?" I asked.

"What do you do?"

"Lots of stuff," Orville said. "We find hidden treasures and become spies and mad scientists."

"Our mission," I explained, "is to make something exciting happen every day."

"I'm in." She set her backpack on the ground.

"Riot Brother Rule Number Twenty-Five: In order to become a Riot Brother, you must take the Riot Brother Oath," Orville said.

She raised her right hand.

"Very good," I said. "Now flare your nostrils and repeat after me. I, say your name, promise to save another brother from the clutches of boredom . . ."

She stood tall and flared her nostrils. "I,

say your name, promise to save another brother from the clutches of boredom . . . ," she said.

It was an oldie but a goodie. Orville fell down laughing.

"Sorry," Amelia said. "Couldn't resist." She raised her hand and flared her nostrils again. "I, Amelia E. Hart, promise to save another brother from the clutches of boredom . . ."

". . . by thinking of fun things to do with my enormous brain."

". . . by thinking of fun things to do with my enormous brain."

Even though that should have been the end, Orville added, "And if I ever find a lot of money on the ground, I promise to buy Orville some candy."

"And if I ever find a lot of money on the ground, I promise to buy Orville some candy," Amelia repeated.

"And share it with Wilbur," I added.

"And share it with Wilbur," she repeated.

We taught her the secret Riot Brother handshake. (Don't tell anybody, but the directions for this are printed in the back of this book.)

"You are now a Riot Brother," I said.

"So what's our first mission?"

"We are going to solve a mystery. The only problem is, we haven't found one yet."

"I love mysteries!" Amelia put her aviator hat in her backpack and put on her mystery-solving hat. "That's better. Now, let's get cracking. Do you have any mysterious places around here?"

Orville jumped right in. "That place on Garfield Road where the women put their heads in those electric helmets is very mysterious."

"That's Bertha's Beauty Salon, Orville. I think the electric helmets are just hair dryers."

"Oh." Poor Orville looked disappointed.

"Wait a minute! The shed! Mom keeps

blaming us for leaving the door open, but we haven't been in there. So that means someone else is leaving the door open."

"Perhaps we should investigate," Amelia whispered.

"The shed is dark and creepy," Orville warned. "And it smells like dried slug juice."

What does dried slug juice smell like, you wonder? Come over and smell our shed.

"The creepier the better," Amelia said.

"Let's bring Slobber and Curly," I suggested. "If someone is in there, we can throw them at him and scare him out."

"Fake pets." Amelia sighed affectionately. "They're always there when you need them."

FIVE
A Tempting Trap

We took Amelia behind the garage to see the shed, and guess what?

Did you guess that a giant slug was blocking the entrance? Well, that would've been sweet. But you'd be wrong. We found that the door was wide open, which wasn't as interesting as a giant slug, but still was pretty interesting considering it was supposed to have been closed.

"We must investigate," Amelia whispered.

We crept into the shed.

"What are we looking for?" Orville whispered.

"A clue of some kind that will tell us who is using this shed and what they are using it for," I said. "Too bad we didn't bring our flashlights."

Amelia pulled a flashlight out of her backpack.

Orville and I looked at each other.

"That girl knows how to pack," Orville said.

On one side of the shed was the lawn mower and big gardening tools. On the other side of the shed were our sleds and our old red wagon.

"Is anything missing?" Amelia asked.

Orville kneeled down and peered under the wagon. "Shine your light down here, Amelia. I think I see something."

We kneeled next to Orville. Hidden under the wagon was a pile of gloves.

"There's Mom's missing purple glove and

my missing goalie glove!" I said. "Look! There's Mrs. Overhoser's missing blue glove. And wait a minute! Isn't that the glove Mr. Lawson uses when he polishes his car?"

"Looks like we have a mystery on our hands!" Amelia said. "Someone is stealing gloves and hiding them in your shed."

Orville wiggled his fingers mysteriously. "A glove lover!"

I inspected the pile. "It's a thief who steals only one glove in a pair. Perhaps it's a one-armed thief who needs them to hide his fingerprints!" I suggested wisely.

Amelia pulled a magnifying glass out of her backpack and peered closely at the pile. "Let's look for clues."

Orville sniffed. "Whoever the thief is, he or she smells like a banana split."

"Actually, that's me," Amelia said, pulling a slightly rotten banana from her pack.

After she turned her attention back to the glove pile, she found something. "Look at

this! A black hair. And another. Our thief must have black hair!"

"Nice detective work, Amelia," I said, and she beamed.

"Let's set a trap," she suggested.

"Great idea!" Orville exclaimed. "I'll get the cheese!"

"O-bro, we're not setting a mousetrap," I explained. "We're setting a glove-thief trap. We'll put a pair of gloves in a strategic spot and then hide and watch to see who steals one. Right, Amelia?"

"Right!"

Orville shrugged. "Maybe we should put some cheese there, too. In case it's a thief who likes cheese."

How could you argue with that?

The first thing we had to do was get some cheese because just thinking about it made Orville hungry. But we didn't have to go far because guess what? Amelia had some in her backpack. "I like cheese," she said.

Next we had to get a pair of gloves. But we didn't have to go far because guess what? Amelia had a pair of black-and-red batting gloves in her backpack.

"Wow!" Orville exclaimed. "You got any ice cream in there?"

"Sorry." Amelia shrugged. "It would melt." Her face lit up. "Hey! A portable personal freezer to fit in a backpack pouch would be an excellent invention." She took a little notebook out of her backpack and jotted the idea down.

We set the gloves on a tree stump near the street, got our binoculars, hid behind the bushes, and waited in the hot sun. Amelia crossed her legs, put her fingers on her

temples, and closed her eyes. We waited. And waited.

"Have you ever noticed that when you want people to walk by, they don't?" I whispered.

"It's like the ice cream truck," Orville whispered back. "It never comes when you really need it."

"Hold on," Amelia whispered. "I'm almost done meditating." She rubbed her temples with her fingers and whispered, "Send us a suspect. Send us a suspect." She opened her eyes. "Look!"

Jonathan Kemp came out of his house carrying his piano book.

"Works every time!" Amelia whispered. "Here's our first suspect."

"Nah, it's just our friend Jonathan."

"He's on his way to his piano teacher's house," I said.

Amelia began rubbing her temples again. "Send us a suspect. Send us a suspect."

Mr. Overhoser walked by.

"What about him?" Amelia asked. "He only has a few hairs left."

We watched closely. Mr. Overhoser glanced at the gloves, but kept walking.

A black cat crossed the path next.

"Uh-oh," Orville said. "Bad luck!"

"Here's what you do to reverse bad luck," Amelia said. She turned around, put her thumb on her nose, wiggled her fingers, and counted backwards from seven. "Works every time."

We all did it.

Then we turned back around, and I peered through the binoculars. Only one batting glove sat on the tree stump.

"The thief has

struck again!" I exclaimed. "A glove is gone! Someone must have run by while we were reversing our bad luck. Whoever it is must have been watching us to know when our backs were turned."

"What bad luck!" Orville moaned. "Wait a minute. I thought we were reversing our bad luck. I'm so confused."

Amelia jumped up. "It's good luck! See? We wanted the thief to strike again so we could catch him . . . or her."

I jumped up. "Of course! The thief will re-turn to the shed to put the new glove in the hiding place, so if we go back and hide near the shed, we should be able to solve the mystery."

Orville jumped up. "Hooray! Let's go!"

The next thing we all said was "Ouch!"

Why?

Because we were so excited, we bumped right into each other.

SIX
Stick 'em Up!

We tiptoed behind the garage and noticed that the shed door was slightly open.

"Didn't we close that?" I whispered.

Amelia and Orville both nodded.

"The thief has already returned," Amelia whispered.

We tiptoed closer and closer.

We could hear a faint noise, the sound of someone moving around inside.

I don't know about Orville and Amelia, but my heart was beating as fast as popcorn popping.

"What should we do?" Orville whispered.

Amelia pulled Curly out of her backpack and spoke up in a loud, strong voice. "We know you're in there! We've got you surrounded."

"Yeah." Orville pulled Slobber out of his pocket. "We have animals here, ready to bite you."

"I need something to hold," I whispered. Amelia nodded and threw me the banana.

I held it out and said loudly, "We also have rotten fruit. So come out with your hands up! Or, if you only have one hand, come out with that up."

There was no sound.

"Open the door," I whispered to Orville.

"You open it," he whispered to Amelia.

"Wilbur should. He's the oldest," she whispered.

"Let's all do it together," I suggested.

In slow motion, we put our hands on the door and opened it wider and wider and wider. . . .

Crouched in the darkness by the wagon, looking right at us, was . . .

A pair of glowing yellow eyes!

Orville yelped and threw Slobber.

Amelia yelped and threw Curly.

I yelped and threw the rotten banana.

The thief screeched and bolted between our legs.

What kind of thief has yellow eyes and can run between the legs of short people?

A cat burglar! A black cat burglar!

We chased after the cat, who ran all the way to Ms. Booth's house and hid in her bushes.

"That figures," Orville said as we caught our breath. "Ms. Booth is crazy about cats."

She answered after three knocks.

"Hello, Ms. Booth. We're here because we believe that one of your cats has been stealing gloves," I explained.

"It's a black cat, ma'am," Amelia added.

"Who really has a thing for gloves," Orville added.

"Meatball?" Ms. Booth asked.

"No thanks," Orville said. "We just had some cheese."

"No. Meatball is the name of my black cat. She's been missing for several days now," Ms. Booth said.

"Well, she's hiding in the bushes right here." Amelia pointed.

Ms. Booth brought out a bowl of food and tapped it. "Meatball! It's din-din time!"

The cat came out of the bushes and started chowing down.

Ms. Booth clapped her hands. "Oh, I was so worried. Thank you for finding her. And sorry about the gloves. She's always had a thing for gloves."

"No problem, ma'am," Amelia said. "We're very good at solving mysteries."

"You might want to buy Meatball some gloves of her own," Orville suggested.

Ms. Booth blew us kisses and took Meatball inside.

"Looks like we did it!" I said as we headed home. "In fact, we triple-did it! We solved the mystery of who was leaving the shed door open and who was stealing gloves, and we solved a mystery that we didn't even know was a mystery: the mystery of the missing Meatball."

"Three mysteries in one!" Orville exclaimed.

"Hip hip, hooroonie!" Amelia cried and threw her hat in the air.

Then the three of us did a victory dance.

SEVEN
Pass the Peas, Please

It was fun returning the gloves and explaining how we caught the cat culprit. Everybody congratulated us, and Mrs. Overhoser was so glad to get her favorite gardening glove back she even gave us cookies!

The rest of the day went by very quickly. We introduced Amelia to our neighborhood friends—Margaret, Jonathan, Alan, and Selena—and played with them.

Then Mom called us in for dinner. "We're having pasta and peas," she said.

"Peas!" Orville started jumping up and down. "We love peas!"

Amelia elbowed me. "What am I missing?"

"We invented a dinner table game using peas, called Holey Cheese-n-Peas. Orville particularly loves it because he usually wins."

She nodded. "I have a feeling I'm going to like it."

After we ate our pasta, we put a big slice of cheese on each of our plates.

"How many holes this time?" Orville asked me.

"How about five?"

We punched five perfect holes out of each cheese slice by using a drinking straw's rim like a cookie cutter, and then we passed the straw to Amelia so that she could do the same.

"Okay, now put five peas on your plate, anywhere except in the holes."

"Got it," Amelia said.

"When I say go, we will all pick up our plates and try to get the peas to land in the holes by tilting the plate around. We have one minute. After the time is up, whoever gets the most peas in the holes wins."

Amelia grinned and held on to her plate, ready for action.

"Go!" I said.

Mom watched the time.

Plates tilted. Peas rolled.

"Yes!" I got one.

"Pretty please, little pea, go in the hole," Amelia said.

"Yes! Yes!" Orville cried. He must've gotten two.

"Hooray!" Amelia got one.

"Ten seconds left," Mom said. "Nine, eight, seven, six . . ."

My peas wouldn't stay put.

"Yes! Yes!" Orville cried.

"Yes! Yes!" Amelia cried.

"Five, four, three, two, one! Time's up!"

"Whooeee! I have all five!" Amelia was so excited, she jumped up and all the peas flew off her plate. "Well, I *had* all five."

"I'm a witness," Mom said. "She did have all five."

"Sorry," Amelia said to Orville.

"That's okay. I'll get you next time!" Orville said with a grin.

Amelia did a little victory dance.

"Okay, now eat your peas!" Mom said.

We ate the peas. We ate the cheese. We even ate the holes.

"You know what I always say? Somehow

food tastes better after you've had the chance to play with it," Amelia said.

"That's a Riot Brother saying if ever I heard one," I said. "May we add that to our Riot Brother saying collection, Amelia?"

"I'd be honored," she replied.

When it was time for bed, we set up the cot for Amelia in our room.

Mom said good night, told us to go to sleep, and went downstairs to play her cello.

It was too hot to be under the covers, so the three of us were lying on top of our covers. I couldn't see either Orville or Amelia, but I could feel them.

As I listened to the sound of Mom tuning up downstairs, I thought about how much fun it is to have another person sleep over. It's sort of like getting a new member of the family for a night.

I dug my handy flashlight from under my pillow and turned it on. (Riot Brother Rule #19: Always keep a flashlight under your pillow.) "Hey, Amelia," I whispered. "We have a confession to make."

"We do?" Orville turned on his flashlight.

Amelia leaned over the cot and pulled her flashlight out of her backpack. "What is it?"

"We thought you would be boring."

She laughed.

"It's true," Orville said. "Sorry about that."

She shrugged. "I thought you'd be boring, too. Here, watch this." With her flashlight in one hand, Amelia made a shadow puppet of a snake on the wall with her other hand. I made my hand into a dog and howled. Then Orville made a snake that slithered over, ate my head off, and burped.

Amelia laughed. "That looks like Curly." She gasped. "Curly! And Slobber! We left them in the shed."

"Along with that rotten banana," Orville added.

"Hmm." I shined the light under my chin so that it made my face look all spooky. "Per-

haps we should sneak into the dark of the night and retrieve them."

Amelia and Orville both grinned.

As quietly as three giant slugs, we grabbed our flashlights and crept down the stairs and out the back door. The air was warm and still. The moon was full and ghostly white.

Amelia stopped. She lifted her arms to the moon and sang in a soft, mysterious voice, "Full moon, full moon, make something funny happen to us soon." She dropped her arms and explained, "If you sing a tune to the full moon, your wish will come true."

"I've never heard of that," Orville said. "I wonder if something funny will happen." Then he tripped over the garden hose.

We all laughed.

Amelia shrugged. "See? Works every time."

"Come on," I whispered.

Our flashlight beams bounced off the grass and our bare toes. Amelia started giggling because the grass was especially tickly.

We tiptoed to the shed and opened the door. The tools and sleds looked creepy in the dark.

"Curly? Where are you?" Amelia whispered.

Orville shined his light on the lawn mower. Curly was draped over the handle.

"There you are!" Amelia rescued him.

Orville found the stinking banana in the

sled and threw it out the door. Slobber was hiding in a flowerpot.

"I'm thinking that Curly needs one more adventure before hitting the hay," Amelia said.

"I like the way you think," I said. "What do you have in mind?"

"We could put her in the bathroom sink, and when your mom goes to brush her teeth—"

"*Ahhhhhhh!*" Orville acted out the scream in a whisper.

Amelia giggled again.

"We've put Slobber under her pillow, but never a snake in the sink," I said. "She won't be expecting it."

We closed the shed door and began creeping back across the yard.

Orville laughed his evil laugh. "*Moi-ha-ha!* This is going to be fu-u-u-un." His foot slid out from under him, and he hit the grass with a thunk.

"What happened?" Amelia asked.

Orville shined his light on a smooshed mess. "Who would put a rotten banana right here?"

"A Riot Brother with a very short memory," I said.

"Oh." He laughed.

We helped him wipe the banana goop off. Then we crept in, put Curly in the bathroom, and snuck back to our room.

Planning a clever joke on someone you love is fun. Carrying it out is even more fun. And waiting for the response is even more fun. As we were tiptoeing up the creaky stairs, I was filled to the brim with happiness. The summer was just beginning, and already we were having a great time.

Meeting a new cousin that turns out to be someone really fun is like finding a million dollars.

"Good night, Amelia," I whispered. "Good night, Orville."

"Good night, Riot Brothers," she whispered back.

I closed my eyes and began to fall asleep.

Let me tell you, there's nothing like drifting off to sleep after a fun-filled day and hearing the beautiful shriek of your dear mother finding a snake in the sink.

The End

ONE
Tut, Tut, Nut

I woke up nice and early and knew without even looking that Orville and Amelia were still asleep. How did I know? Because they were both snorgling like wild pigs. As anyone who has ever had a sleepover at my house knows, Orville does more than snore—he snorgles. And now you know that Amelia E. Hart snorgles, too. Up until this point in my life, I didn't even know that girls *could* snorgle.

I glanced at them to see if they looked like wild pigs.

They did!

I really wanted to take a picture of them so that I'd have something to look at whenever I needed a laugh, but I had to follow Riot Brother Rule #13: Whoever wakes up first has to wake the other. And according to our new rule, I couldn't wake them up in an ordinary way.

Riot Brother Rule #26:
If you have to wake
up someone,
be creative about it!

I crept downstairs and got the mop bucket. Quietly, I tiptoed back upstairs and filled it with whitey-tighties, socks, and fluffy white tissues. I climbed on my bed and held the bucket in both hands as if it were very full of water. (It helps to be a good actor.) Then I said, "Yoo-hoo. Orville, Amelia, time for a shower!"

Amelia opened her eyes and saw me standing above them with that big old bucket.

"Orville!" she said. "Wake up!"

Orville's eyes snapped open. "Wilbur! You wouldn't—"

"Here it comes!" I tossed the contents of the bucket at them.

"NOOOOOOO!" They covered their heads.

An avalanche of white socks and under-pants and tissues landed on them.

I laughed my head off.

Pow! Amelia got me right in the forehead with a sock ball.

"Sock fight!" I cried.

Orville started throwing socks in both directions like a wild, two-handed pitching machine.

When we were socked out, Amelia sighed and said, "What a way to start the day! You guys know how to do it."

"Thank you, Amelia," I said. "It's nice to be appreciated."

"It certainly is," Orville said, and put a pair of whitey-tighties on his head.

"That gives me an idea!" Amelia exclaimed. "Let's play Costume Countdown! You get one minute to use anything you can find to create a costume. Then we guess what we are." She didn't wait to find out if we wanted to play. Why would she? Of course we did! She pulled a stopwatch out of her backpack. "You may get something from another room, but you must be back here in one minute. On your mark, get set, go!"

The three of us raced around, grabbing stuff and putting it on. We ran back.

"Time's up!" she said. "Okay, guess what I am."

She was standing very straight and was wearing Curly the snake wrapped around her right arm, a T-shirt on her head like a scarf, and a fake beard.

"A fortune-teller?" I guessed.

"No."

"Santa Claus's evil twin?" Orville guessed.

She laughed. "No. I am the great Egyptian queen Nefertiti!"

"A queen with a beard?"

"Yep. When she became the pharaoh, she wore a fake beard! Isn't that cool?"

"Do me next!" Orville yelped. He was wrapped in toilet paper with my striped tie around his neck.

"You're a daddy mummy!" Amelia said.

"I can't believe you got it right!" Orville exclaimed.

Amelia bowed.

A chill went up my spine. "This is very strange."

"What's so strange?" Orville asked.

"You'll see after you guess who I am."

I had a pair of whitey-tighties on my head with two tissues sticking down on either side.

"You're a sheep?" Orville asked.

"Baaaaad guess," I said.

"Give us a hint," Amelia said.

"I'll tell you that I'm a rich king, but you'll have to figure out my name."

"Oh my gosh!" Amelia exclaimed. "This *is* strange."

"What?" Orville asked.

"He's King Tut!" Amelia said, and I nodded. "He looks just like him." She pulled a book called *Egyptian Wonders* out of her backpack. "See? Here's King Tut, except he's painted gold."

Orville jumped up, made a King Tut hat for himself, and danced like an ancient Egyptian with his mummy bandages trailing. He sang:

I'm the richest guy: King Tut, Tut, Tut.
I live in a palace, not a hut, hut, hut.
I've even got a golden—

"Orville," Amelia said. "Sorry to in-terrupt your song, but don't you see how strange this is?"

He stopped.

"What's so strange?" Orville asked.

"We all picked costumes from ancient Egypt," I explained.

"I think it means that our mission for today must have something to do with Egypt," Amelia said. She started jumping up and down. "I love ancient Egypt!"

Orville's costume was giving me a great idea for a mission. "What would be a cool thing in the world to find?"

"A dollar?" Orville guessed.

"Cooler."

"An air conditioner?" Amelia reasoned.

"Well, that would be cooler. But that wasn't what I had in mind. I think our mission should be to find a lost mummy!"

"Bingo bongo!" Orville started singing:

We're going to find a mummy like Tut, Tut, Tut! I know 'cause I can feel it in my gut, gut, gut.

He stopped. "You know what King Tut should do?

"What?" we asked.

"Make a mini putt!" Orville said. "He could decorate it with miniature pyramids and call it King Tut Mini Putt! It's a great idea. Let's go visit King Tut and tell him about it, and he'll give us a bunch of gold as a reward!"

"There's only one problem." Amelia patted him on the back. "King Tut is dead."

"That is so sad." He plucked the tissues out of his hat and blew his nose. "No mini putt for King Tut."

I said to Amelia, "When you've got a brother like Orville, there's only one thing to do. . . ."

"Put on a King Tut hat and be a nut, nut, nut?" she suggested.

"Bingo bongo!"

TWO
Dung Beetles, Anyone?

What is the first thing to do once you've decided that your mission will be to find a lost mummy?

Notify the newspaper? Fly to Egypt? Dig a tunnel in a pyramid?

Wrong.

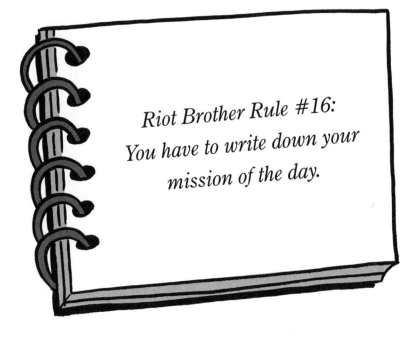

Riot Brother Rule #16:
You have to write down your
mission of the day.

We showed Amelia our Secret Riot Brother Mission Book.

"Let's invent our own Riot Brother Hieroglyphics to write down our mission!" she said.

I was beginning to think that there just might be another person in the world with almost as many great ideas as myself.

Here's what we came up with:

Translation:
The Riot Brothers will find a lost mummy.

The next step was to pack.

I bet you're dying to know exactly what you need if you're going to search for a lost mummy.

Well, here's the list:

THINGS YOU NEED FOR
A MUMMY SEARCH

1. Flashlight for peering into spooky tombs.
2. Explorer's helmet to protect your head from falling cobras.
3. Toothbrush for dusting dust off sarcophagus.
4. Magnifying glass for looking at scary mummy face.
5. Camera for taking picture of mummy.
6. Running shoes for running away from angry mummy.
7. Candy for eating because Orville likes candy a lot.

We got dressed and put on our fastest running shoes. As for everything else on the list . . . guess who had it all in her backpack?

You're right. Amelia!

We headed downstairs, Amelia first, then Orville, then me.

"Wait!" Amelia stopped.

Orville crashed into her, and I crashed into Orville.

"We need one more thing before we go!" she said.

"Breakfast?" Orville asked.

"Okay, we need breakfast, too. But first we must go on a bug expedition."

Orville was beside himself with joy. "I don't know what an expedition is, but I love anything with bugs!"

I, being older and wiser, said, "An expedition is a search."

"Correct," Amelia said. "We must search for a dung beetle!"

Orville made a face. "To eat for breakfast?"

"I think I get it," I said. "The dung beetle was considered a magic charm in ancient Egypt. Am I right?"

"Bingo bongo," Amelia said. "Ancient Egyptians carried around dung beetles called scarabs to protect them from angry ghouls and spirits. We should, too."

Orville sighed. "Those ancient Egyptians knew how to have fun."

We ran into the front yard and began digging. We found lots of worms, but no beetles.

"Our problem is that we don't have any

big rocks to look under," Orville said. "Bugs like living under big rocks."

There is one person in our neighborhood who has nice big rocks lining his driveway. I knew who it was. And Orville knew who it was. But Amelia didn't. Do you? I'll give you a clue. He's big and mean, and his name is Goliath Hyke. Our neighborhood bully.

We explained the situation to Amelia.

Amelia listened. "I have my ways of dealing with bullies," she said.

So we tiptoed over to Goliath Hyke's house. The driveway was empty. The shades were drawn. Either everybody was asleep or nobody was home.

"Not a creature is stirring," I whispered. "Not even a mouse."

"Or even a rat," Orville added.

We crouched and lifted up the nearest rock. What do you think we saw? One bug? Two?

A whole city's worth of creatures were scurrying around. Earwigs, springtails, snails, and worms! Nematodes, spiders, slugs, and pill bugs! And beetles? Bazillions of beetles!

"Probably even mites," Orville whispered. "What a beautiful sight."

"I agree." It was beautiful to see all these different little guys, with all their strange-looking body parts, going about their business underneath this rock. It makes you glad to be alive. And big.

"Hello, little buggies," Amelia whispered. "Which one of you would like to come and help us with our mission? We promise to bring you back."

Orville scooped up a nice shiny beetle. "Why doesn't everybody love bugs? They're so cool."

We watched the beetle scurry around the palm of Orville's hand.

"Just think," I said. "If we had a microscope, we could see another city of even smaller creatures in the dirt."

Amelia nodded. "And maybe there's somebody on another planet, looking through a telescope at us."

We all looked up to the great glorious sky . . . and yelped.

There was Goliath Hyke looming over us.

"That's MY rock!" Goliath yelled.

All the creatures scurried out of sight, probably feeling very glad at that moment to be small.

Goliath grabbed me by the shirt. "WHAT ARE YOU DOING WITH MY ROCK?"

It's a tiny bit hard to think fast when a boy who looks like he would eat you on toast for breakfast is holding you by the shirt.

Goliath tightened his grip. "TELL ME!"

My life began passing before my eyes, which was a bad thing because that usually means you're about to die. On the other hand it was a good thing because I've had a very entertaining life.

Amelia stood up. "My name is Amelia E. Hart. I am an entomologist, as well as an explorer with a great knowledge of ancient Egypt. I am searching for a scarab along with my partners, and I am not accustomed to being yelled at in this manner."

Speechless, Goliath let go.

Amelia turned to Orville. "Now, Orville. I believe the bug you're holding is, indeed, a scarab, otherwise known as a dung beetle. It is precisely the bug we need."

"If—if you f-found it under my rock, it's mine," Goliath stammered gruffly.

"I see," Amelia said. "Then you know it is a rare poisonous biting scarab. One bite from this and blood will ooze from your palms and then your brain will turn into slush and drain down through your nostrils!"

Orville tossed the beetle in the air, and

Amelia caught it. She held it out to Goliath. "Would you like it?"

Goliath scowled. "If it's so poisonous, how come you're not afraid to hold it?"

Amelia pointed to her backpack. "I have the antidote in there."

Goliath looked at us, wondering if he should believe her.

"Trust me," Orville said. "She's got everything in there."

"Give me the antidote *and* the bug," he growled.

"Certainly," Amelia said. "But you should know that, although the antidote will save your life, it cannot take away the pain. Right, guys?"

I nodded. "Horrible pain."

"Truly horrible pain," Orville added for emphasis.

"I don't believe you," Goliath said.

Just then, Amelia screeched, "Ack! I've been bit!" She threw the bug back at Orville, dropped to her knees, and howled. "Oh, the pain!" She slapped her hands together and writhed. "Oh, the truly horrible pain!" She opened up her hands. Blood was oozing all over her palms.

Goliath took two steps back. "Uh, maybe I should get my mom. . . ."

Amelia turned to look at us and gave us a secret Riot Brother wink. Then she moaned. "The antidote, Wilbur! Quick!"

I knew just what to do. I rummaged through her backpack until I found something to eat. "Aha, the antidote!" I pulled out a small box of raisins. "We discovered that a chemical in raisins is the antidote. Remember, Orville?"

"I hope so, because Amelia looks like she's going to die."

I tried to feed her a raisin, but she rolled and moaned.

"Amelia!" I said. "You must eat the antidote!"

"I'm—I'm going to get some help." Goliath started to leave.

Quickly Amelia snapped a raisin out of my hand and popped it into her mouth. After one and a half chews, she sat up and let out a big groan. "I'm alive! Thank goodness, the antidote worked."

Goliath looked at Amelia, then at Orville, then at me. I could tell he wasn't sure what to believe.

I found the beetle in the grass and held it

out to Goliath, along with the box of raisins. "As long as you have raisins handy, you'll be okay."

"Who needs a stinking bug," he said, and ran.

Let me tell you, watching a bully run away is as beautiful as finding bugs under rocks.

Amelia hopped up, grinned, pulled a handkerchief out of her backpack, and wiped the blood off her hands.

Now it was our turn to be speechless.

She pulled a package out of her pocket. "Fake blood capsules. Just slap your hands together and it oozes blood. You should always carry one around— you never know when you're going to need it."

We agreed that Orville's pocket was a good place to carry the scarab. "I've got plenty of cracker crumbs in there if it gets hungry," Orville said.

"Let's name it Scary the Scarab," I suggested.

"Excellent idea," Amelia replied. "Are we ready for an adventure?"

"Bingo bug-go!" Orville said.

THREE
Toot, Toot, Tootsies

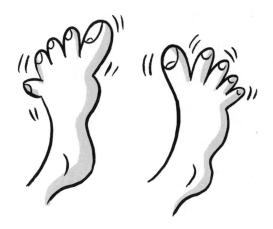

Here is a question for you. How clean are your toes? Ours are the cleanest toes on the entire planet.

You may be wondering why I am talking about toes. Well, you'll find out soon if you just keep reading.

After our successful scarab expedition, we ran into our house to plot our next move.

"We have everything we need," Amelia said, "so let's get cracking."

"Where do we go to find a lost mummy?" Orville asked. "Egypt?"

"Too expensive. Not enough time," Amelia answered.

"How about a cemetery?" I suggested.

"Brilliant!" Amelia exclaimed.

Getting a compliment from your own brother is nice. But when a new cousin notices your brilliance, it makes you feel good all the way down to your clean—or dirty—toes.

We were just about to go find a cemetery when Mom stopped us. "Just the kids I was looking for," she said. "I'm going to take you to the history museum. There's an exhibit on—"

"NOOOOOOOOOOOOOOOOOOOOOOO!" I cried.

"But there is a fascinating exhibit on—"

"Mom!" Orville pleaded. "We don't have

time. If we spend all day at a museum we'll never have time to . . . "

"To what?"

I elbowed Orville. He couldn't tell her our mission. *(Riot Brother Rule #2: Do not tell anyone your true mission.)*

Mom was waiting for an answer. "Orville, if we go to the museum, what won't you have time to do?"

Some people get ideas from their brains. Orville gets his from his feet. He looked at his feet and said, "We won't have time to scrub our toes, of course! We were looking forward to spending a long time on it."

"You want to scrub your toes?" Mom looked doubtful.

Orville nodded and stuck one foot in the air. "We put on our running shoes before washing our feet, which was a big mistake."

You're probably wondering what I was thinking. Well, I was thinking that poor

Orville had come up with a clunker. No way would our mom believe that we were planning to scrub our feet.

But before Mom could say anything, Amelia jumped in. "It was my idea. Our feet really are in need of freshening up, which is why it's so great that I brought my homemade foot scrub." She pulled a jar of green goop out of her backpack. "It contains peppermint, green tea, thyme, and Dead Sea salt. My mom and I make it ourselves. It exfoliates and invigorates."

Mom laughed. "Wow. I thought I'd heard everything. Well, I guess you better go wash your feet, then."

We couldn't believe it! We were off the hook.

But then she stopped us. "After you scrub your feet, you can put your shoes back on, and then we'll go to the museum. Clean feet *and* a field trip." Mom grinned. "What a way to kick off the summer."

We marched into the bathroom.

"I never thought I'd spend time on the second day of fun and freedom washing my feet," I admitted.

"Sorry," Orville said. "It was the first thing that popped into my head."

"Don't be sorry. Foot scrubs are fun!" Amelia chimed in.

I looked at Orville, and Orville looked at me. Sometimes one brother can tell what another brother is thinking. Orville could probably tell that I was thinking, Hmmm, maybe, just maybe, our cousin Amelia doesn't always have the best ideas, after all. As for Orville . . . he was probably thinking about candy.

Anyway, we took off our shoes and got our feet wet, then she put a dollop of her foot scrub onto each foot. It was goopy and gritty, but it smelled so minty and delicious I was a little nervous that Orville would try to eat it.

"Rub and scrub, boys!" Amelia said. "Nothing like clean feet."

We rubbed and scrubbed the goop into our feet and toes.

"Wow!" Orville cried. "My feet love this stuff!"

I could feel the ingredients sinking into my skin cells and exfoliating with vigor. It didn't feel just good. It felt fabulous.

Orville starting scrubbing his toes with a toothbrush and singing,

This little piggy went to Egypt.
This little piggy went to France.
This little piggy ate peppermint.
This little piggy lost his pants.
This little piggy went on an
expedition inside a volcano and got
all covered with hot lava and died.

We laughed.

Mom came in. "Orville! It's disgusting to use your toothbrush for that."

"I'm not using my toothbrush," he said. "I'm using yours. And my little piggies love it!"

Mom made Orville's little piggies march over to his little piggy bank. He had to give her his own money to buy a new toothbrush.

"Oh well," he said. "It was worth it. Our feet have never looked, smelled, or felt so good."

We washed off the goop, and I looked

down at my gleaming toes. "I got to hand it to you, Amelia. You can even make foot washing fun."

Amelia wiggled her tootsies and took a bow.

"Unfortunately, we will have to put our mission on hold while we go to that museum."

Amelia put the foot goop back in her pack. "I was just thinking that a history museum might be the perfect place to find a lost mummy. Maybe there's a basement in the museum or a storage closet that no one has looked in for a long time. We could—"

A rustling noise and a thunk came through the open bathroom window.

Thankfully my reflexes are extremely quick. I ran to the window and peered through the blind.

"Someone was spying on us!" I exclaimed.

"How can you tell?" Amelia asked, peering out the window. "Did you see somebody?"

"No, but look!" I pointed to our recycling

bin, which had been turned over and put directly under the bathroom window. "The spy used our bin to stand on so that he or she could listen in through the open window."

"Why would someone be spying on us?" Orville asked.

Amelia frowned. "No doubt it is another explorer who wants to find the lost mummy before we do and take all the credit."

"Either that," Orville said, "or it's somebody who likes to hear me sing about my toes."

"Come on," I said. "We're going to be the ones to find a lost mummy, or we aren't the Riot Brothers. Let's get to that museum before the spy does."

FOUR
I Want My Mummy

"MOM!" Orville yelled. "Let's get rolling!"

"Wow," Mom said. "I didn't think you were that eager to go."

"We are!" Orville said. "We can't wait. If we don't go this minute we're going to explo—"

I nudged Orville. Sometimes he can go just a bit too far.

The phone rang. "Well, let me get that," Mom said. "And then we can go."

While our mom answered the phone, we

ran to the front door and stopped dead in our tracks. An envelope was sitting by the door. Someone had pushed it through our mail slot while we were busy washing our feet.

"Looks like the mail came," Orville said, picking it up.

"But the mail already came today," I said.

Orville flipped it over so we could see the writing on the front.

It was addressed to Amelia E. Hart!

Amelia gasped. "Who would be sending me a letter?"

"Open it and we'll find out," I suggested. "But be careful in case we have to dust it for fingerprints later."

Carefully, Amelia opened the envelope. "Look," she said. "It's a word scramble."

Fifteen squares of paper were in the envelope, each with one letter of the alphabet printed on it.

"I think it's a riddle," Amelia said. "We're supposed to put the letters together to form words to solve it."

"It must be a message from the spy," I said.

"Either that or from somebody who likes to play word games," Orville said.

We spread the letters out and stared at them.

Let me just take a moment here to say how thrilling it is to get a secret riddle through your mail slot when you are on a mission of epic proportions. If the message was from a spy who wanted to beat us to a lost mummy, I had to admit that I liked his style.

"I see a word," Amelia said. "Look." She took five of the letters and formed the word *GHOUL*.

A shiver ran up my spine.

I moved the letters around until a cool five-letter word popped out. *"Sooty!"* I exclaimed.

"Excellent adjective!" Amelia said.

"Okay," Orville said. "It's my turn to make a word. Nobody say anything." He stared at the letters and then he jumped up. "I got one!" He pulled one letter out of the pile and set it down. *"A!"*

"It may be little, but it's still a word," I said. "So we have *a sooty ghoul* so far."

We stared at the remaining four letters. Amelia moved them into place. *"Live. A sooty live ghoul!"*

"Or . . ." I rearranged the first four letters. *"Evil. A sooty evil ghoul!"*

"What does it mean?" Orville asked.

"I think it means we're on to something big," Amelia said. "There is probably a filthy evil ghoul guarding the lost mummy. The spy whose mission is to get there first probably wants to scare us off with this message."

Orville rubbed his hands together. "This is going to be good."

Mom walked in. "Now I'm ready to go," she said.

"So let's step on it," Orville said.

Mom laughed.

Unfortunately we never got the money to actually manufacture our one-of-a-kind Riot Brother Carpeted Carjet, which is a car that turns into a jet and has very plushy carpeting. So we had to drive to the museum the regular way. Fortunately, it's not a long drive.

Before we could sing all the way down from "100 Jars of Foot Scrub on the Wall," we were pulling into the parking lot. A big banner across the museum entrance read, EXPEDITION TO EGYPT: SECRETS OF THE TOMBS!

We were stunned by our good luck.

"Wow, Mom," I said. "Why didn't you tell us it was an ancient Egypt exhibit?"

She shrugged. "I tried."

Guys dressed up like pharaohs were showing us where to park, and the people taking the tickets were dressed up like Egyptian gods and goddesses.

"Look, there's Queen Nefertiti!" Amelia exclaimed.

This museum knew how to do it.

We went inside. There was another exhibit on Rome, which Mom made us roam through first. Finally, we got to the Egyptian exhibit.

The first room was filled with all sorts of cool objects. Orville pointed to a jar with a lid shaped like the head of a jackal. "That would make a cool cookie jar."

"That's a canopic jar," Amelia said. "It was used to store a dead person's stomach."

Orville's eyes popped out. "If we ever go

to Egypt, let's pack our own snacks. Okay, Wilbur?"

"Check this out." I pointed to a whole case full of scarabs made out of gems.

Orville whispered into his pocket, "Hey, Scary, you're famous!"

"Wilbur," Mom asked, "why is Orville talking to his pocket?"

"Doesn't everybody?" I asked. And then I told my pocket to be quiet and pay attention.

Amelia pulled our arms and whispered with great excitement, "Look!"

We did what any Riot Brother would do. We looked without looking as if we were looking.

What did we see?

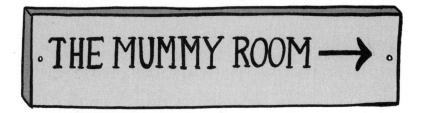

"Let's go!" Orville said.

FIVE
Stares and Stairs

Mom was busy reading every little sign in every little room. We told her that we wanted to go ahead in the exhibit, and she agreed to meet us in the mummy room in fifteen minutes.

"Let's take a quick look at the mummy room and then head to the basement and see if we can discover a lost mummy of our own," Amelia suggested.

The mummy room was darker than the other rooms and much spookier, even though it was crowded. Coffins shaped like people were standing up all around; and in a big glass case was a horrible-looking thing badly wrapped in the dirtiest blankets I'd ever seen.

"Man, this guy could use some foot scrub," Orville said.

"She's a real mummy, Orville," I said.

Amelia added, "She's been dug up, so of course she's filthy!"

"How do you know it's a she?" Orville asked.

Amelia and I pointed to the sign: MUMMY, FEMALE.

Orville started dancing. "We found a filthy lost mummy!"

I put my older and wiser hand on his shoulder. "Don't get excited, O-bro."

Amelia nodded. "We haven't succeeded because this mummy isn't lost."

"Get lost," Orville whispered to the mummy.

The mummy didn't say anything back.

We tried to stare at the mummy, but if you've ever seen a real mummy, you know it isn't easy. Mummies aren't exactly pretty to look at. Their faces are all sunken and disgusting.

Orville shivered. "Why do we want to find a lost mummy, anyway?"

"I know what you mean, Orville," I said. "But according to Riot Brother Rule Number Five, we can't change our mission in the middle of the day."

We were about to leave when something strange happened.

Have you ever had the feeling that you were being watched? Orville and Amelia and I all got it at the exact same time.

Of course we were being watched by a security guard, who was dressed like King Tut. (Okay, his hat was a little nicer than ours.) But it wasn't that. Someone else had his eyes on us.

"I think the spy is here," Amelia whispered.

At that very moment, I glimpsed a dark shape slipping out the exit. "Did you see that?" I pointed.

The three of us stood for a moment, feeling the electricity of excitement snap between us. Nothing like being spied on to put a little zing in your mission!

"He might have heard us mention the basement," Amelia whispered. "Let's get there before he does."

Quickly, we walked through the exhibit to the elevators, which were busy. I noticed a sign on a door that said, STAIRS. We stared at it. No doubt they led to a dark and spooky place.

"Let's go as quietly as possible," Amelia said. "He might be waiting for us around any corner. Is Scary ready if we need him to ward off evil?"

Orville peered into his pocket. "Check!"

"You go first, Orville," Amelia said.

"That's okay. Wilbur can go first," Orville said.

I sighed. "All right. We'll all go at the same time."

It took us a while to squeeze through the door all at the same time, but we made it.

The stairwell was empty and dim. We began to tiptoe down the stairs, aware that we had never been in more danger.

Well . . . this seems like a fine place to stop for a chapter break! See you later!

SIX
Even Mummies Need a Break

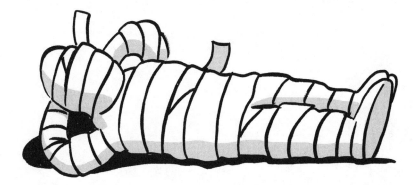

Welcome back! Where were we? Ah, walking down the stairwell.

At the bottom of the stairwell was a door. Cautiously we opened it. The door led to a dim hallway, as quiet as a cemetery, with three doors. Holding our breath with excitement, we tried the first. Locked. We tried the second. Locked. We tried the third. Locked.

We had reached a dead end, which you'd

think would be a good place to find a lost mummy. . . . Get it? *Dead* end. But it wasn't.

The only other objects were a vending machine and several big garbage cans in the hallway. Of course we checked the vending machine.

Riot Brother Rule #27:
Always check vending machines
for loose change or candy.

We were about to go back upstairs when we heard someone coming down the stairs toward us. Our hearts began to pound again. Quickly we hid behind the garbage cans and waited.

I don't know what Amelia and Orville were thinking, but my mind kept drifting back to the vision of that mummy with the sunken eyes.

Orville must have been thinking along the same lines, because he whispered, with closed eyes, "Tell me if it's a lost mummy. I can't look!"

The door from the stairwell opened just slightly. Would it be a member of the living dead, smelling like rotting flesh, walking in to claim us as zombie victims and drag us to the underworld?

Amelia lifted her camera.

A strange odor drifted in through the cracked door. It wasn't exactly rotting flesh. It was more like . . . aftershave.

In walked Goliath Hyke!

I almost fell over. I nudged Orville, who opened his eyes and almost fell over, too.

For a bully, he looked strange. First of all, he was wearing a very nice shirt, the stiff kind that buttons up. Who in their right mind would wear that kind of shirt on summer

vacation? Second of all, he had on sandals. I had never seen him wear sandals. And his feet were extremely clean. To top it all off, he smelled like he had poured a bottle of his dad's aftershave all over his head.

He looked around, and then he turned and walked back to the stairwell. We listened until his footsteps were gone.

"The spy is Goliath Hyke!" I exclaimed.

"And there's something wrong with him," Orville said. "He's not acting like himself. He doesn't even look like himself."

"Perhaps he's disguising himself as a nice guy, thinking that we wouldn't recognize him," I said. I checked my watch. We had run out of time. Mom was expecting us. "Well, we didn't find a lost mummy. But at least Goliath didn't either. We'd better go back."

"What do you guys do if you don't complete your mission?" Amelia asked as we began to climb the stairs.

"I don't know," I admitted.

"If we don't complete our mission, I'm going to cry," Orville said.

Amelia patted him on the back. "There's still time. Maybe we'll find a lost mummy on the way to the—"

Just then we heard heavy footsteps. *Schkunk! Schkunk!*

"Someone's coming down from the second floor," Orville whispered. "It's probably Goliath again."

Schkunk! Schkunk!

"It's probably a security guard who's going to arrest us for being in the basement," Amelia whispered.

"But listen," I whispered. "Those don't sound like normal shoes making that sound. Maybe it's a member of the ancient living dead."

"Only one way to find out," Amelia said.

The mystery person turned the corner and began heading down the stairs toward us. It was a mummy! He was huge and

wrapped in filthy bandages. *Schkunk!*
Schkunk!

We froze, looking at each other. I could
tell that Amelia and Orville were thinking
what I was thinking. If you have ever seen

a mummy in a glass case, you know how spooky they are. But that's nothing compared to one actually walking toward you in a dim stairwell. His arms dangled from their sockets. His eyes stared right through us with a ghoulish blackness. He didn't look like a nice mummy. He looked like the type who puts curses on people and takes their stomachs home in jars.

"Don't worry," Amelia said, trying to control the quiver in her voice. "Scary will protect us."

I didn't want to burst her bubble, but this guy looked like he'd eat Scary as an appetizer.

"We should hide!" Orville whispered.

But the mummy was quick and there was nowhere to hide.

Our Riot Brother legs started to shake.

The mummy was getting closer.

I thought about grabbing Amelia's camera and taking a picture to prove that we had seen him before he dragged us to the under-world, but I was too scared to move.

When he was close enough to touch us, he stopped. "Hey," he said. "Do you guys know where the mummy room is? I'm lost."

We couldn't believe our ears.

"I just started working here," the mummy went on. "And it's really hard to see out of this thing. Is this the door to the first floor?"

"You work here?" Amelia asked, and he nodded.

"He's a nice mummy!" Orville flashed me a huge, relieved grin.

"And a lost mummy!" I said. "Do you know what this means?"

We started dancing around. "We found a lost mummy! We found a lost mummy!"

"Excuse me," the lost mummy said. "Sorry to interrupt your dancing, but I'm supposed to be the guide for that room, and I'm already late."

We escorted the mummy to the mummy room, where our mummy was waiting for us. Goliath was also there, watching us from the corner. He looked very out of breath and red in the face—jealous, no doubt, because we had completed our mission.

"Where have you been?" Mom asked.

"I'm confused, Wilbur," Orville whispered. "Can we tell Mom about our successful Riot Brother missions when we're done?"

"Riot Brother Rule Number Twenty-

Eight," I said. "You may talk about success-ful secret missions after completion."

"Great!" Orville exclaimed. "Mom, we wanted to find a lost mummy and we did! This guy was lost and we brought him back here."

An important-looking woman with a clip-board was listening. "Thank goodness!" She turned to the mummy. "We were worried about you, Harry. Glad you're safe and sound."

The museum director shook our hands, and Harry the mummy thanked us politely.

"For a guy who is supposed to be dead," Orville told Harry, "you have good manners."

"Can you tell I'm smiling?" the mummy asked us.

We couldn't.

"I guess a dead guy can only look so happy," he said.

I nodded wisely and added, "That's true, of corpse."

Now That's the Kind of Lava I Like

"Being a mummy in a museum looks like a fun job," Amelia said as we were getting into the car.

"Yeah," Orville said. "Mommy, may I be a mummy when I grow up?"

Mom laughed.

"You know why mummies need to have

lots of breaks?" I asked. "Because they're all wound up."

Orville laughed.

I was on a roll. "What do you think mummies like to eat for lunch? Wraps!"

Orville laughed again.

Amelia jumped in. "Where do mummies like to go when it's really hot? To take a swim in the Dead Sea!"

Mom groaned and started the engine.

I had another. "What do mummies do when they catch a cold? They can't stop coffin!"

Mom looked at us in the rearview mirror. "What do mommies do when they're tired of hearing mummy jokes?" she asked.

"They buy their children ice cream?" Orville guessed with a big grin.

"No," she said. "They become numby."

I nodded. "Not too crummy, Mummy!"

On the ride home, we invented a new Riot Brother game. As soon as we got home we

ran over to Jonathan's house. Jonathan, Alan, Margaret, and Selena were all outside playing with Jonathan's puppy.

"I bet you're *dying* to learn a new game called the Curse of the Mummy," I said.

Orville cracked up. "*Dying* to play the Curse of the Mummy? Get it?"

"Is it fun?" Jonathan asked.

"It's a riot!" Amelia replied.

Everybody wanted to play, of course.

"Don't look now," Margaret said. "But Goliath is watching us from behind that tree."

I looked without looking as if I was looking. Goliath was hard to miss.

"I think he wants to play," Amelia said. "Should we invite him?"

Our mouths fell open. "Are you crazy? He's the neighborhood bully."

"For a bully, he does have extremely clean feet," Amelia said.

Before anybody could stop her, Amelia walked over and asked Goliath if he would like to play.

The gang was shocked into silence.

"Um—okay," Goliath said. We were ready for him to take over and start bossing us around. But he just looked at Amelia and asked, "How do you play?"

Amelia explained the rules.

"I'll be the mummy first," I announced. "I'm going to put a curse on everybody. Don't forget, you have to try to tag me while acting out the curse." I tried to think of a curse that would make them look really funny and summoned up a deep, scary voice: "May your legs go wobbly forevermore. . . . You will be cursed at the count of four." I wiggled my fingers at them and counted, "One . . . two . . . three . . . four!"

"Ahhhh!" They yelled and writhed as if the curse was running through their veins. With bobbly wobbly legs, they ran after me. I dodged them this way and that. Finally Amelia tagged me.

"Now you get to be the mummy!" I told her.

Amelia thought up a great curse. "May bats fly at your face forevermore. . . . You will be cursed at the count of four." We all ran around screaming and ducking and swatting at imaginary bats.

Everybody had a couple of turns before Mom called us in.

"Well, that new game was a huge success," I said to Orville as we went inside.

"We've had a great day," Orville agreed. "I think that calls for a celebration."

"Uh-oh," Mom said. "What did you have in mind?"

"How about if you make us volcanoes of ice cream with hot fudge lava?" Orville asked.

"Sure," she said.

We couldn't believe it.

"Wow, Mom," I said. "Every once in a while you say something really smart."

She warmed up the fudge and put mountains of ice cream in our bowls. We broke off the bottoms of ice cream cones and stuck them deep in the center of our ice cream mountains to hold the lava.

While we made sound effects, Mom poured so much hot fudge into our volcanoes that they erupted over the sides. Yum!

We dug in with our spoons. For a while we were speechless. Ice cream can do that to a person.

Eventually, Mom made us go to bed.

"I know you're going to want to stay up," she said. "But if you get some sleep tonight, then you can still have some fun tomorrow morning."

She blew kisses, turned out the light, and left.

We waited silently until we couldn't hear any more footsteps.

"Amelia," I whispered. "What are you thinking about?"

"I'm thinking about how hard it must be to go to the bathroom in a mummy costume. What are you thinking about, Wilbur?"

I was just about to answer when we heard a tap at the window.

Our bedroom happens to be on the second floor, so a tap on our window is very unusual.

"Did you hear that?" I asked.

Another tap came.

"Either a blind bird just flew into our window twice," Orville said, "or someone is out there."

We ran to the window.

"There's something in the driveway." Amelia shined her flashlight down. "Come on, more shine power."

We shined our flashlights down, too.

There in the driveway under the window was a bunch of rocks arranged in the shape of a heart.

"Whoa!" Orville said. "Who did that? And why?"

"I think I know," Amelia said.

She pulled the envelope of letters out of her backpack. "Let's just take another look at this message." She tossed the letters onto the floor and we gathered around with our flashlights. First she spelled out A SOOTY EVIL GHOUL. Then she rearranged the letters into a new message:

GOLIATH LOVES YOU

"WHAT!!!" I yelped.

"Since when does Goliath love me?" Orville cried.

"Not you," Amelia said. "Me. I've suspected it for a while now. Look at the clues. Red in the face. Out of breath. Tongue-tied. Nice clothes. Aftershave. Clean feet. It all started the minute he met me. He wasn't spying on us or trying to find the mummy first. He was just trying to be near me."

Orville and I recoiled in horror.

"I don't believe it." Orville sat on his bed. "This is just too much for my little brain to handle."

Mom walked in. "I thought I told you guys it was time for bed."

"Something shocking and horrible is happening," Orville groaned.

Mom flipped on the light. "What is it?"

"Mom," I said, "if I were to tell you that a certain somebody is red in the face, out of breath, and tongue-tied, and that he is also starting to wear nice clothes and aftershave as well as washing his feet—what would you say?"

"I'd say Goliath Hyke is head over heels for your cousin."

I fell over. "*What?* How did you know?"

"You can tell just by looking at him. Poor guy. Besides, when his mom called to ask which museum we were going to because Goliath really wanted to go, I figured something was up."

Orville shook his head. "How do women know these things?"

Reality was sinking in. Goliath was so in love that he was doing embarrassing things, like arranging rocks in the shape of a heart on the Riot Brothers' driveway.

"Wait a minute!" Orville jumped up, his eyes gleaming. "We could really tease him about this!"

Amelia shook her head. "No. You must have pity on his tortured soul."

"I agree," Mom said. "After all, someday it will happen to both of you."

I looked at Orville. Orville looked at me. "NO WAY!!!"

"Well, you don't have to worry about it

right now," Mom said, tucking us all in. "Right now you have to worry about going to sleep." She turned out the light.

I lay in bed, thinking about Goliath's strange behavior. What if Amelia were to fall in love with Goliath? What if they were to get married? Then Goliath would become our second-cousin-in-law and he and Amelia would have very large babies.

"Amelia," I whispered, "I have to ask you something."

"What?" she asked.

"Do you—um—like Goliath in return?"

She was silent for a moment. Then she said, "I'm keeping all my options open."

It was a mysterious statement from a mysterious girl.

"You know what I'm thinking?" Orville said.

"What?" we both asked.

"I'm thinking that we should paint our underpants gold so that they make better King Tut hats."

"Over my dead body," Mom called out.

"Wow," Amelia said. "Your mom has big ears."

Orville nodded. "We've been telling her that for years."

"I heard that," Mom called again. "You can talk in the morning. Now go to sleep."

Amelia fell asleep before we did. How did we know? Because we heard the sound of snorgling coming from her cot.

That girl snorgles like two wild pigs rolled into one.

"Whoever she marries better buy earplugs," Orville said.

And then he fell asleep and began snorgling.

As for me, I was tossing and turning and having a terrible time trying to get to sleep. Then I remembered what Amelia had said about the moon.

I looked out the window and sang in a soft mysterious voice, "Full moon, full moon, help me fall asleep soon."

And I did!

The End

ONE
Gotta Beat the Heat

CRASH!

"Wake up!" Amelia slammed two pot lids together. "It's time for the Riot Brother Weather Report!" She was standing on my bed.

> *My name is Amelia, and I like to snort.*
> *And I'm going to give you my weather report!*
> *Today is not cloudy. No chance of rain.*
> *So play outside,*
> *but don't get smooshed by a train.*
> *Hottest day on record!*
> *You don't need a coat.*
> *But please wear some clothes—*
> *unless you're a goat.*

She gave the pot lids one final crash.

We did what any appreciative audience would do. We clapped. "That was a creative way to wake us up."

"Thank you. And it's all true." Amelia jumped down. "Your mom said it's supposed to be the hottest day on record."

"Hey!" I exclaimed. "Let's go to the Splash-and-Soak Water Park."

"Bingo bongo!" Orville started hopping

around. He couldn't help it. When he gets excited, he just has to hop.

Mom walked in with a laundry basket full of clean clothes. "Forget it. Amelia's parents are coming to pick her up this afternoon."

"We could go in the morning," I suggested wisely.

"It's too expensive," Mom said.

Orville sighed. "Why are you always worried about money, Mom? Live a little!"

Mom laughed.

"Wait!" Orville cried. "I know where we can get the money. Who always has what we need in her backpack?" He grinned and held his arms out to our cousin.

"I do have a collection of money." Amelia began pulling stuff out of her pack. "Let's see. I have several ancient Chinese coins. I'm sure they are very valuable in China. Some Swiss francs, Japanese yen, and Chilean pesos. Sorry, Orville. I guess I'm short on American cash."

"But you're big on personality." Mom laughed.

"Hey, Mom, if we make enough money, will you take us?" I asked.

"I doubt you could make enough," she said.

I grabbed a sheet of paper and drew a one hundred dollar bill. "Here! I just made some."

Amelia and Orville thought it was funny, but my own mother ignored me. "While you're thinking of more schemes," Mom said, "you can put away your clothes." She dumped the clean laundry on the floor.

"We will put away our laundry for a price," Orville said.

Mom put her hands on her hips. "In your dreams, buster!"

"Why are you so grumpy?" Orville asked.

"I'm not grumpy!" she said.

"You're grumpy because it's so hot today," I said. "It's so hot, if we don't go to a water park, our poor cousin will melt."

Amelia melted dramatically to the floor.

Mom laughed. "I'm not grumpy!" She took the empty basket and left the room

to go do whatever it is that grumpy mothers do.

I sat next to Orville, who was looking grumpy himself. I wasn't feeling grumpy at all. That's because I had a plan. "Orville, have we ever failed in any of our missions?"

"No."

I smiled at Amelia. "It's true. So, let's make it our mission to have fun at a water park. That means we'll succeed. And how will we succeed? Simple. We will use our amazing brains to come up with a money-making scheme. If we make enough money, Mom will be impressed and agree to take us."

"But according to Riot Brother Rule Number Two, we cannot tell anyone our true mission," Orville said.

"So let's not tell Mom that it's our *mission* to do it. We'll just raise the money and ask for a ride."

"I like it!" Amelia said. "But we'll have to get rich quick!"

"We can do it!" Orville hopped into our pile of clean clothes like it was a pool of water. "Water park, here we come!"

TWO
Please Don't Eat the Ham

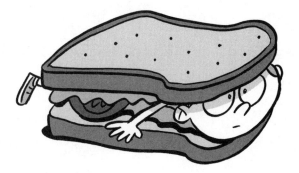

"This will be easy," Orville said. "All we have to do is sell people something they need. Then we'll make a lot of money. What does everyone need?"

"Cheering up," Amelia said. "Let's brainstorm things that cheer people up."

"Candy!" Orville started hopping around again. "Let's buy a bunch of candy and sell it to people."

"There's only one problem," Amelia said. "We need money to buy candy."

Orville stopped hopping. He looked so sad I wanted to cheer him up. Then I wondered, what besides candy always cheers Orville up? My brain started storming, and from a tornado of thoughts, one image came flying out: a puppy. "How about something with puppies?" I suggested. "Puppies cheer you up."

"Puppies!" Orville started hopping again. "We can borrow Jonathan Kemp's puppy and take it door-to-door! We can charge people one dollar to pet the puppy, and it won't cost us anything."

I made Orville hop over to the phone and call Jonathan Kemp to see if we could borrow his puppy.

I don't know about you, but I don't like making phone calls. I can never think of what to say because I'm always thinking about what the other person is going to say. Orville has it easy. He just doesn't think.

While he made the call, we watched his

face. It went from hopeful to hopeless in three seconds. "Jonathan's mom said no," he said after he hung up. "She *lives* with a puppy and she's still grumpy. That's just not right."

"We can't give up!" Amelia cried. "Let's keep our brains storming. What else cheers people up?"

Orville whirled around as if the storm in his brain had turned into a hurricane. "I got one!" He stopped. "Pirates always cheer themselves up by singing songs."

"I love pirates!" Amelia said. She pulled a pirate hat out of her backpack and put it on.

Now it was my turn to be a hurricane of ideas. "We could go door-to-door selling songs! Our neighbors will gladly empty their pockets to have their day brightened with the joy of music! I can play my tuba!"

"I can be the percussionist." Amelia grabbed the two pot lids and smashed them. *CLASH.*

"Hip hip, hooray!" Orville cried. We all whirled around the room, and then we crashed into each other like lightning bolts and fell down. "But wait!" Orville said. "I don't have an instrument yet. What should I do?"

"You can be the singer," I suggested. "I happen to know that you can make up songs on the spot."

Orville grinned and sang,

I can sing on the spot. I'm funny!
I can sing when it's hot and sunny!
So please pay us a lot of money!

This was going to be great.

To be more efficient with our time, we split into groups. Orville and I worked on advertising in the den. Amelia disappeared into the kitchen to create a "portable percussion outfit."

We made a big poster advertising our service, but then we realized that it would be hard to carry around.

"I could wear it," Orville suggested.

"That idea gives me an idea." I made another poster. Then I attached strips of cardboard to join the two signs together and slipped the whole thing over Orville's head. He looked fabulous.

ONE
DOLLAR
FOR A SONG!
HOW CAN YOU
GO WRONG?

Mom walked in. "You've made a sandwich board," she said.

"What?"

"That's what it's called when you have two advertisements back-to-back like that."

"I get it," I said. "The posters are two slices of bread, and Orville is the ham!"

"Orville certainly is a ham," Mom admitted.

"Rats! Somebody already invented it?" Orville asked.

"Well, I think you're the first to invent a sandwich board to sell songs," Amelia said.

We turned and saw her in the doorway. And what a vision she was.

Over her shorts and T-shirt, she was wearing a skirt made of spatulas and slotted spoons. She had pot lids strapped to her knees  and another on her head like a beret. In her right hand she had a large wooden spoon, and in the other she held a plastic mixing bowl turned upside down. In addition to all that, she was wearing an eye patch and had her left arm in a sling. "Ready?" she asked, and banged the lids on her knees together.

"Wow," Mom said.

"Thank you for letting me borrow your kitchen utensils. I will take good care of them." She adjusted the patch over her eye. "The eye patch and the sling are mine. If people think I've been in an accident, they might give us more money."

"Brilliant!" I exclaimed.

"Maybe you should put some blood all over you," Orville suggested.

Mom cut us short. "You don't want to scare people. I think you're good to go just as you are."

"Wait," Amelia said. She struggled to put her backpack on. "You never know when you might need something. Besides, I feel naked without it."

I hoisted up my tuba. Orville adjusted his sandwich board. And off we went.

Mom called out: "Remember, you're only

allowed to go to the houses of people we know."

Lucky for us we're famous. We know everybody on our block, and everybody knows us. We decided to see our neighbors Dan and Karen Doorley first. They just had a new baby who cries all the time. They could definitely use a cheering-up song.

We walked to the Doorleys', or rather we clanged. It was hard for any of us to walk normally. The burning heat marched right along with us. It was so hot you wouldn't even need a toaster to make toast.

We knocked, and Dan peeked through the little window at the top of the door. He looked like he hadn't slept in days. He whispered something, but we couldn't hear him.

Orville spun around so that Dan could read the back of his sign.

Dan's eyes got really big, and he made some kind of hand motion. He was definitely excited.

"What did he say?" Orville asked.

"I think he's telling us it's too hot to open the door, so we should play extra loud," Amelia said. "Ready? Hit it!" She banged her knees together to give us a beat.

I honked out a tune on my tuba.

At the top of his lungs, Orville sang,

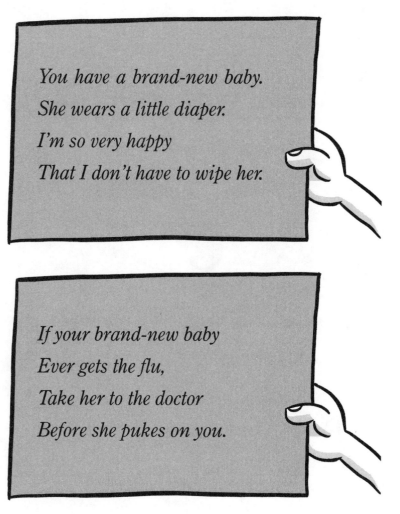

You have a brand-new baby.
She wears a little diaper.
I'm so very happy
That I don't have to wipe her.

If your brand-new baby
Ever gets the flu,
Take her to the doctor
Before she pukes on you.

I honked out a big *tada* sound at the end, and Amelia hit the pot lid on her head with the wooden spoon.

You could tell that Dan had never experienced the joy of having musicians come to cheer him up right at his door. He was in shock.

There was one moment of silence. And then behind him we heard a very loud *WAAAAAAAAAAA!*

"I think we woke the baby," I whispered. I

could tell by the way Dan's teeth were clenched that this was not a good thing.

"Do you think we should ask him for a dollar?" Orville whispered.

"I think we should run before he calls the police," Amelia whispered back.

"Sorry!" we said. And then we ran.

Our other neighbor's mean dog howled behind his fence.

"That's Doom," Orville explained as we huffed and puffed down the street. "The Dog of Death."

"I think Doom likes our music," Amelia said.

"If our only fan is Doom," I said, "we're doomed!"

We ran as fast as three kids wearing a tuba, sandwich sign, and cooking supplies can run on the hottest day of the year.

THREE
Double Trouble

"I wish this heat would go away," Orville cried, wiping the sweat from his brow.

"Wait." I felt a saying coming on. *"Weather* should be spelled *whether,"* I said, "because you're stuck with whatever *weather* you've got, *whether* you like it or not."

"So true," Amelia said.

I led the way toward the Overhosers' house. Mrs. Overhoser was out gardening, as usual.

"Not the Overhosers!" Orville whispered. "They're mean and crabby!"

"Exactly. They *need* us."

We marched up the path.

"Don't be stepping on my pansies!" she yelled.

"Why would we step on her pantsies?" Orville whispered.

"Not *pantsies*. *Pansies*," Amelia explained. "It's a kind of flower."

I nudged Orville. "Tell her why we're here."

Orville twirled around so that she could read the back of his sign. "We're here to offer you a song."

"I've never heard of such a thing," she said, adding a dandelion to a big pile of weeds.

"It only costs one dollar," Amelia added. "Guaranteed to cheer you up."

"Just a minute," she said, and left.

The sweaty singing sandwich started to panic. "Is she going to call the police?"

She came back with a dollar. "Do you know the song 'Wild Blue Flower'?" she asked.

We shook our heads.

"How about 'Red Is My Rose'?" she asked.

"Sorry," Orville replied.

I pointed to the flowers lining the walkway. "You obviously love pansies, Mrs. Overhoser. My talented brother will make up a beautiful song about pansies just for you. Won't you, Orville?"

Orville nodded. "For a dollar, I'll do just about anything."

Amelia clinked her spatulas, I tooted out a few notes on my tuba, and Doom howled along in the distance. Then Orville began to sing:

There was a field of pansies loved by an Overhoser. And then one day they got killed by a big bulldozer.

Mrs. Overhoser gasped.

Amelia and I looked at Orville.

"Sorry, it just came out." He shrugged. "Sometimes rhymes seem to have a mind of their own."

Mrs. Overhoser's eyes began to get watery, and I don't think it was because of allergies.

"I'll cheer you up." Orville tried to bend down to pick her a flower, but his sandwich board got in the way and he fell . . . flattening a whole row of pansies.

Poor Mrs. Overhoser sat in the grass, stunned with sadness.

We gave her the dollar back and left.

"I don't think we exactly cheered her up," Amelia said.

"Look, there's Mr. Lawson washing his car." I pointed. "Let's try singing something happy to him about cars," I suggested. "That seems safe."

"Got it!" Orville said.

To get to Mr. Lawson's house, we had to pass Goliath's house, and there was Goliath sitting on his front steps, tossing a football from one hand to another.

"Goliath is going to make fun of us," I whispered. "Pretend you don't see him. Just keep walking and don't pay any attention."

Every muscle in my body was preparing for the firing of insults from Goliath's mouth.

"Hi, Goliath," Amelia said as we approached his house.

"Hi," he replied.

"We're selling songs," she said.

I knew what was coming next. He was going to tell us how lame it was to try selling songs.

"I would like to buy a song," Goliath said. "But I don't have any money. Would you take this in return?" He held out his football.

Orville and I couldn't believe our ears.

"Love makes you do crazy things," Orville whispered to me.

"We couldn't possibly take your football," Amelia said. "If you stay outside, you can enjoy our songs for free. We're really loud."

"Okay," he said.

"Let's go, boys," Amelia said.

Stunned, we walked on.

Amelia sighed. "Poor Goliath. He wouldn't be so miserable if he didn't love me so much."

We walked up to the Lawsons' house.

"What do we have here?" Mr. Lawson said, turning off his hose.

Orville turned around to show off our sign. "A dollar for a song."

"That sounds like a great deal," our neighbor said. "Especially since you found my missing glove." He took off his work gloves and pulled a crisp one-dollar bill out of his wallet.

Ah, that dollar was like a cool breeze refreshing our weary spirits.

"We will play you a song about your car," Orville said.

"Honey, come and hear this!" Mr. Lawson called out. His wife came out with a frying pan.

As soon as we started playing, Doom wailed along. He really did seem to love our music.

Orville started singing:

You have a cool red car—
The best thing in your life.
You love it so completely,
Your car should be your wife.

I didn't wait to see if Orville had a second verse.

"Sorry about that," I said, and handed back the beautiful crisp dollar bill.

Mrs. Lawson turned to Mr. Lawson and waved her frying pan at him. "Do you love that stinking car more than me, Edward?"

"Of course not, sweetie!" Mr. Lawson said. "Don't listen to that crazy boy."

"Yes," Amelia said. "Don't listen to him."

"I'm completely bonkers!" Orville stuck his tongue out the corner of his mouth and flapped like a dodo bird.

"Come along, crazy cousin." Amelia pulled Orville back toward our house.

"Well, I have learned something," he said after we were out of earshot. "I have learned that songwriting is a dangerous business. Rhymes get me in trouble."

"Double trouble," I said. "Look who's coming after us."

Doom had jumped his fence and was heading straight for us.

"Run!" I yelled at Orville.

We ran. Again.

We jumped over hedges and slid between parked cars and cut through a big pile of mulch and finally made it home, huffing and puffing. We ran inside and closed the door.

Then we realized something terrible.

Amelia wasn't with us!

Orville covered his eyes. "I can't look! Tell me, Wilbur. Does she have any arms or legs left?"

I peered out the front door. Amelia was standing right where we'd left her. Doom was snuggled in close to her, wagging his tail.

"She's petting him!" I yelped.

Orville looked.

From his front steps, Goliath was staring, too.

Nobody in the history of the neighborhood had ever been brave enough to pet Doom.

Amelia led Doom back to his house. A few minutes later, she was back.

"Doom really does love our music," Amelia said.

"Did you try selling him a song?" Orville asked.

"No. But his owner gave me a dollar for bringing him back." Amelia grinned and held up a crisp dollar bill.

FOUR
Did You Say, "Croak"?

Mom walked in. "You boys are filthy! Don't take another step inside this house."

"It's not our fault," Orville protested, taking off his sandwich board.

"Whose fault is it?"

Orville sighed. "It's a messy world, Mom. We just happen to live in it."

"Hose off outside," she suggested, which wasn't a bad idea.

We took off all our song-business gear and turned on the hose.

"Let's take a break and teach Amelia one of our famous Riot Brother Water Games," I said. "How about Croak-and-Soak?"

"Do I like it?" Orville asked.

"You love it, Orville. You invented it! Orville is great at inventing games," I explained to Amelia, "but not so great at remembering them."

I reviewed the rules. When I explained that she and Orville would get to be the "croakers" and that croakers are frogs, she exclaimed, "I've got a frog hat!"

Orville turned to me. "It's too bad that Amelia only has one head because she sure does have a lot of hats."

I had to agree.

As soon as she put it on I stood in the center of the yard with my eyes closed, holding the hose. Orville and Amelia ran around the

yard, croaking like frogs. Every time one of them croaked, I tried to spray the person with the hose without looking. You can tell that you've hit the target if the croak turns into a scream.

We took turns croaking and soaking until we were delightfully drippy.

"Well, I'm as clean as Mr. Lawson's car now," Orville said.

That gave me a great idea. "Let's have a car wash. People will pay us to clean their cars."

"It's a great idea," Amelia said.

Orville shook his head. "But according to Riot Brother Rule Number Five, you can't change your mission in the middle of the day."

"Our mission is to have fun at a water park. It doesn't matter how we earn the money to get there," I explained.

"Well then, what are we waiting for?" Amelia said.

We made another sandwich board sign advertising our car wash and put it in front of our house.

"Maybe we should invent a Riot Brother Car Washing Machine to make it more fun," I said.

"Let's invent a robot that walks around the car and washes it," Orville suggested.

"How about a robot dressed like a frog that

says ribbit?" Amelia said. She got out her notebook and began sketching. "We could call it the Ribbot."

"Guys," Orville exclaimed, "I think we make a great team!"

FIVE
It's Raining! It's Pouring!

What do you do if you don't have time to build a robot from scratch? You turn Orville into one. We started with swim trunks and Amelia's aviator goggles. Then we added flippers on his feet, rubber gloves on his hands, and—best of all—a lawn sprinkler strapped to a bicycle helmet, strapped to his head.

"Wait behind the fence," I said. "As soon as a car arrives, I'll say *ready*. That will be our code word. When you hear *ready*, turn on your sprinkler, come out, say *ribbit* in a robot voice, and start scrubbing."

"Ribbit," the robot said, picking up a bucket of water and sponges. "I'll be ready for *ready*. But I can't see very well with these goggles."

"It's okay," Amelia said. "Just give the car a good soak."

Orville hid behind the fence, and Amelia and I waited by the curb for customers.

Margaret came over to see what was going on. Goliath watched from afar.

Finally, a car drove up. It was Jonathan Kemp's mom, with Jonathan and Tiffany in the back.

"Hello, Wilbur," Mrs. Kemp said as they hopped out of their car. "Are you trying to earn a little extra money?"

"Actually, we're trying to earn a lot of extra money. Would you like our amazing robot to wash your car?"

"A robot? Cool!" Jonathan said.

"That sounds great," she said, pulling out a dollar. "Are you ready for a customer?"

Sometimes it does not pay to have big ears. Orville heard Mrs. Kemp say *ready,* so he came charging out with the sprinkler on his head going at full blast. Great twirly streams of water were spurting out.

"Orville!" I cried, but he was saying *ribbit* so loudly he couldn't hear. He was obviously having trouble seeing, too, because he just started throwing sponges. Mrs. Kemp screamed. A sponge bounced off her arm; another bounced off the top of her head.

I ran to the side of the house and turned off the water.

"Ribbit?" Orville said, and took off his goggles.

Everybody stared at Mrs. Kemp.

You know that awful feeling you get when a grown-up is yelling at you? Well, we were bracing ourselves for it when she started laughing. "That was fun!" she said.

"You're not mad?" Jonathan asked.

"It's so hot today, it actually felt good." She wiped the water from her face. "Keep the dollar! And here's a tip."

I couldn't believe it. Now we had three dollars.

In case you're wondering, a wet dollar bill feels just as good as a dry one when you get to hold it in your hot little hand.

"Hey, can I get splashed?" Margaret asked. "Even if I don't have a dollar?"

I looked at Orville and Amelia. I felt a Riot Brother saying coming on.

"You can have fun making money," I said. "And you can make money having fun. But if you have to make money to have fun, you're no fun." I pulled my marker out of my pocket and changed our sign from The Riot Brother Car Wash to The (Free!) Riot Brother People Wash.

Everybody cheered.

"Turn me on full blast!" Orville said, adjusting the sprinkler on his head.

I turned Orville back on and Margaret and Jonathan stepped right up to get soaked and splashed.

Quickly Amelia and I went to work. We got another hose, more buckets, a watering can, a ladder, our old baby pool, a shower curtain, and a blow-up raft and turned the whole yard into a splashy, soaky party scene.

Alan and Selena came and joined in the fun. We played Croak-and-Soak and other water games.

More kids came. "Hey, what's going on?" one of them yelled.

"It's the Riot Brothers Water Park!" Alan yelled back.

Everybody cheered for us.

I pulled Orville and Amelia aside. "Did you hear that? Do you realize what is happening?"

"We're having fun?" Orville gurgled happily.

"Yes, Orville. That means we have succeeded in our mission!"

"We have?"

"Of course!" Amelia patted us both on the back. "Our mission was to have fun at a water park. Although we didn't make enough money to go to the Splash-and-Soak Water Park, we definitely invented our own water park right here, and we're having fun."

"You're right. Hip hip, hooroonie!" He threw an armful of wet sponges in the air.

Ah, nothing like having big wet confetti landing on your head to make your day complete!

SIX
Slimy Gifts

As you can tell, even though it was the hottest day on record, it turned out to be pretty cool for us. We splashed and soaked until we almost croaked. Then our friends went home, and we got a picnic lunch and stretched out on our big lawn chairs in the backyard for a well-deserved break.

"I think our water park was better than the Splash-and-Soak," Orville said as he washed down his peanut butter sandwich with some nice cold milk.

"Yes," I agreed, feeling another Riot Brother saying coming on. "Why buy a ticket to an amusement park when you can ride your own brain for free?"

"Hey!" Amelia said. "We have three whole dollars to spend. We got two from Mrs. Kemp and one from Doom's owner. What should we spend it on?"

"Ice cream!" Orville said.

Have you ever had a moment in your life that was just perfect? Well, we were about to have one.

"I have an idea," Amelia said. She closed her eyes, rubbed her temples with her fingers, and whispered, "Send us an ice cream truck. Send us an ice cream truck." She opened her eyes. "Come on, guys."

We closed our eyes, rubbed our temples with our fingers, and whispered, "Send us an ice cream truck. Send us an ice cream truck."

In the distance, I began to hear a wonderful tinkling sound. I opened my eyes. Amelia and Orville opened their eyes.

The tinkling sound grew louder and louder.

"It's the ice cream truck!" Orville screamed, and fell out of his chair.

"Hip hip, hooroonie!" I yelled.

"Works every time," Amelia said.

We ran to the front and bought ice cream bars and then we ran back to our picnic spot and ate them. Let me tell you, nothing tastes as good as ice cream from a truck on the hottest day of the year.

Just as we were slurping up the last bites, Mom came out and ruined our happy mood with bad news.

"Amelia's mom and dad are here."

"Quick," Orville turned to Amelia, "hide!"

Mom laughed, and Amelia's parents walked out.

"Hey, kiddos." Amelia's dad shook our

hands. "Nice to see you guys again. Last time you were tiny."

Amelia's mom gave us kisses. But when she went to Amelia, Amelia held up her hand. "DON'T KISS ME! I think I have a disease that requires me to stay here for a few more days," she said in a very exhausted voice, and then she slouched in her chair.

"That must mean she really had a good time," Amelia's mom said to our mom. "She only gets diseases when she doesn't want to come home."

Although we tried convincing them to stay, they said they were pressed for time. Their taxi was waiting.

While Mom went to get Amelia's bag and Amelia changed into her traveling hat,

Orville and I ran inside to get a last-minute gift for our cousin.

We all met in the front, where the cab was waiting.

"Amelia, here is a token to remind you of us and the adventures we've had," I said, and handed her a paper lunch bag.

"Is it something delicious to eat?" Amelia asked.

"Nope," Orville said.

She peered into the bag and gasped. "You're giving me Slobber?"

Her parents looked at each other. "Slobber?"

Amelia pulled out our pet rat.

"We wanted to give you something really special," Orville said.

"We know you'll take good care of him," I added.

"Wow," Amelia said. "This is the best thing anybody has ever given me. But I can't take it—he's your only pet."

"We want you to have him," I said.

"How about just for a while . . . until we see you again?" Orville suggested.

"That's a deal," Amelia said. "Here . . ." She pulled some gum out of her backpack. "I haven't even chewed this yet. If you miss Slobber, stick it all in your mouth and chew it really fast, because then you'll slobber and that will remind you of him."

"Thanks again!" Amelia's dad ushered them into the taxi. "Come visit us in Kansas."

"Okay," Orville said, and began trying to squeeze into the backseat.

"Uh—we didn't mean to come visit us right now," Amelia's mom said. "How about sometime soon?"

"Oh." Orville looked as sad as I felt. It was hard saying good-bye to such a fun cousin.

We stood in our yard and waved until the taxi was just a speck in the distance.

"Look over there," I whispered to Orville.

Orville looked without looking as if he was looking.

Goliath was standing in his front yard, waving after the taxi, too.

The taxi turned the corner and disappeared from sight.

Goliath saw us looking at him and yelled, "What are you two dorks looking at?"

"Well," I said, "I guess it's back to normal around here."

Mom made us clean up the mess from our water park. Then we had a lonely dinner and played outside until dark.

At bedtime, our room seemed empty without Amelia.

Mom came to tuck us in.

"When can we go to visit Amelia?" Orville asked.

"I'm not sure," she said. "But I'm glad you guys got along so well."

"Well," I said, "speaking of money, I think you owe us a lot for all the hard work we did today, Mom."

"I wasn't speaking of money."

"Now you are. And speaking of money, I think you owe us a lot for all the hard work we did today, Mom."

She laughed. "Oh? And what did you do?"

"We cleaned and washed everyone in the neighborhood, including ourselves and even Mrs. Kemp. And we watered the garden while we were at it."

"Yeah, you should pay us big bucks," Orville added.

"In your dreams," Mom said.

Orville sighed. "I think I'll dream about money tonight. Wouldn't it be nice if dreams always came true?"

"Sometimes they do. I had the two of you, didn't I?" She gave us each a kiss.

"Aw," Orville said. "For a mom who doesn't give us money, you're not too shabby."

"Gee thanks." Mom laughed, turned out the light, and went downstairs.

"I miss Amelia. And Slobber," Orville whispered.

"Me too," I said with a yawn. It had been a long, busy day, and I was already beginning to fall asleep.

"I'm going to meditate," Orville whispered. "Send us a new pet. Send us a new pet. Send us a new pet. . . ."

I yawned and scooched around, trying to find the perfect position, when my foot touched something cold.

If your foot ever touches something cold

in the bottom of your bed, be afraid. Be very afraid.

I jumped up, tossed off my sheet, and yelped. There was a snake in my bed!

Orville turned on the lights, and Mom came running in.

Curly was curled up at the foot of my bed with a little note attached to her.

Please take care of Curly.
I know she'll like staying with you
for a while.
Love, Amelia

"We have a new pet!" Orville exclaimed, picking her up and kissing her.

"Wow," Mom said. "I never thought I'd see anybody actually kiss a snake."

"Well," I said. "There is nothing like getting a fake snake from your favorite cousin to make you feel all warm and slithery inside."

"Bingo bongo," Orville agreed.

The End

BONUS!

RIOT BROTHER GAMES

Pufferbelly Pointer Punt

First, get your fingers to make some popcorn. You may eat some, but if you eat it all then you can't play the game and you are a Pufferless Pig. Next, make up a name for your "team." Don't get too excited. You don't really have a whole team. You just have your two pointer fingers, but—hey—they're good sports. Okay, now stand across from your opponent at a table and put a piece of popcorn, otherwise known as a puffer, in the center of the table. Say, "Go!" Your goal is to make a goal.

How do you make a goal? You must try to hit the belly of your opponent with a puffer by flicking it with your pointer finger across the table. If you do this, you get a point and

your fingers get to do a victory dance. It ain't easy, though, because your opponent will be going for the puffer at the same time. If you flick your opponent's finger rather than the popcorn, that's a foul and your opponent gets a free kick. If you flick a puffer off the table, your opponent gets a free car! Just kidding.

Whatever you do, don't argue with your opponent because grown-ups make you stop playing if you argue. Just have fun. Whoever has the most points wins. But the winner has to sweep up all the popcorn off the floor, so it's okay to lose!

Holey Cheese-n-Peas

At last, a game requiring skill that you can use to play with peas! Put a piece of sliced cheese on a plate or in the bottom of a bowl. Using a straw like a little cookie cutter, cut out as many holes in the cheese as you'd like. Five or six is usually good. Put several peas on the plate and tilt the plate around, trying to get the peas to land in the holes.

After one minute, whoever has the most peas in the holes wins. The winner gets to decide how many peas the loser has to eat. Ha!

If you happen to be alone, you may play

this game against yourself. Just keep trying to beat your old record. But if you can't beat your old record, then you must eat peas for breakfast for the rest of your life. Ha-ha!

Costume Countdown

You can play this game with any number of players. Everybody gets one minute to use anything (cereal boxes, toilet paper, old clothes), to create a costume. After the minute is up, try to guess what each person's costume is supposed to be. Special advice: If you put a cereal box on your head, make sure it is empty first.

The Curse of the Mummy

This game is best played just as it's getting dark. One

person is the mummy. The mummy gives everyone a curse, using this ancient curse formula.

May _____ forevermore. . . .
You will be cursed at the count of four.

For example,

May <u>your right leg fall off</u>
forevermore. . . .
You will be cursed at the count of four.

After saying the curse, the mummy counts out loud, "One, two, three, four!" During this time, everybody must act as if the curse is coming true. On the count of four, everyone must try to tag the mummy while continuing to act cursed. For example, if the curse was that your right leg falls off, you must hop on your left foot. Whoever tags the mummy gets to be the mummy next.

This game is especially fun if the mummy dreams up funny curses, such as: May your toes curl up. . . .

It also is more fun if the people who are cursed do a lot of great acting with lots and lots of sound effects.

Whatever you do, don't play this game with a real mummy because real mummies are dead, and dead people have no sense of humor. Ha ha ha!

Croak-and-Soak

This game is best played on a hot day, when you're dying for a way to cool off. One person—the soaker—stands in the center of the yard holding the garden hose with his or her eyes closed. The other players—the croakers—run around the yard croaking like frogs. The soaker must try to spray the croakers, using only hearing as a guide. Once you've hit a frog three times, that croaker gets to become the soaker. The croakers must try to

make it difficult for the soaker by moving constantly.

The game ends when everybody is hungry or when the yard turns into a swamp. After the game is over, turn off the hose, pretend it is a microphone, and tell frog jokes, such as this one: How does a frog feel when he breaks his leg? Unhoppy!

The person who tells the most jokes is voted the Croaker Joker. Ha ha ha ha!

BONUS WATER GAMES

The next two games are the "other water games" that we played in the water park story.

Water Limbo

You play limbo by trying to walk under a gradually lowering stick without touching the stick or falling down. You play Water Limbo by trying to walk under a stream of water. The sprayer sprays the hose in a steady stream. Everybody else goes under it while singing the "Water Limbo Song," printed on page 225. Anybody who won't sing has to go home and take a nap.

Put—the—Tail—on—the—Whale

This game is much more fun than pin-the-tail-on-the-donkey. You need at least three people to play this game, but it's fun with more. If you're it, you hold the hose, close your eyes, and count to ten out loud. Everybody else links arms in a chain to form a giant whale. The first person is the head, and the last person is the tail. The whale swims quietly around the person who is it until he or she is done counting. Then, with eyes still closed, the "it" person tries to hit the rear end part of the whale with water from the hose. It's one of the few games where being a rear end is the best part.

RIOT BROTHER SAYINGS

—Somehow food tastes better after you've had the chance to play with it.

—*Weather* should be spelled *whether,* because you're stuck with whatever weather you've got, *whether* you like it or not.

—You can have fun making money. And you can make money having fun. But if you have to make money to have fun, you're no fun.

—Why buy a ticket to an amusement park when you can ride your own brain for free?

ADDITIONAL RIOT BROTHER RULES

Riot Brother Rule #24: Kids who are fun can become Riot Brothers even if they aren't our brothers.

Riot Brother Rule #25: In order to become a Riot Brother, you must take the Riot Brother Oath.

Riot Brother Rule #26: If you have to wake up someone, be creative about it!

Riot Brother Rule #27: Always check vending machines for loose change or candy.

Riot Brother Rule #28: You may talk about successful secret missions after completion.

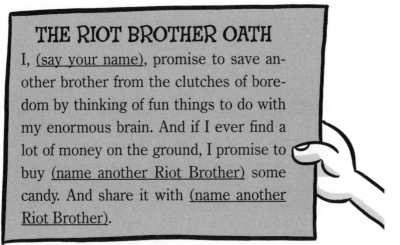

THE RIOT BROTHER OATH

I, (say your name), promise to save another brother from the clutches of boredom by thinking of fun things to do with my enormous brain. And if I ever find a lot of money on the ground, I promise to buy (name another Riot Brother) some candy. And share it with (name another Riot Brother).

THE SECRET RIOT BROTHER HANDSHAKE

Shake right hands (keep holding). Next shake left hands (keep holding). Whisper, "Riot Brothers Rule!" and let go when you say "rule." Slap right hands and grunt. Slap left hands and grunt. Put your right thumb on your nose and wiggle your fingers while you say "I'm no . . ." and knock your left fists together and say "fool!" Practice this so you can do it to a fast rhythm and you'll look cool.

BONUS SONGS

Pointer Anthem

by Wilbur and Orville Riot

O say, can you see, our point-ers with glee? What so proud-ly they stand, as a part of the ha-nd. With their knuck-les they bend; they're the thumb's clos-est friend. They help us to write by hold-ing our pen-cils. They point out the way; they can wig-gle and sway. Al - though they can't snap, they are quite good at tap-ping. O say do they brave-ly dig wax out of our ears. So let's raise our num-ber ones! Now this an-them is done!

The New Baby Song

Do you know a couple with a new baby? Singing this song for them makes an excellent gift. Please change the words to *he* if the baby is a boy. If the baby is an orangutan, you may use *he* or *she,* but don't forget to bring bananas.

Water Limbo Song

by Wilbur and Orville Riot

Don't be a bim - bo. Do the wa - ter lim - bo.

Shim-my, slide, and strut. And don't fall on your... co-co-nuts!

Who invented the Riot Brothers, anyway?

MARY AMATO has written many books for children. Besides the Riot Brothers series, she is the author of the *The Word Eater*, which appeared on numerous state lists, *Please Write in This Book,* and *The Naked Mole-Rat Letters*. Amato lives with her family in Maryland.

ETHAN LONG is a popular illustrator and animator for children. He recently illustrated Holiday House's first graphic novel, *Wuv Bunnies from Outers Pace* by David Elliott, which *Kirkus Reviews* called "perfectly pitched to its audience." He lives in Florida with his family.